Charles T. Hudson

The Rotifera or Wheel-Animalcules

Charles T. Hudson

The Rotifera or Wheel-Animalcules

ISBN/EAN: 9783337419516

Printed in Europe, USA, Canada, Australia, Japan

Cover: Foto ©Andreas Hilbeck / pixelio.de

More available books at **www.hansebooks.com**

THE ROTIFERA;

OR

WHEEL-ANIMALCULES,

BOTH BRITISH AND FOREIGN.

BY

C. T. HUDSON, LL.D. Cantab., F.R.S.

ASSISTED BY

P. H. GOSSE, F.R.S.

SUPPLEMENT.

WITH ILLUSTRATIONS.

LONDON:

LONGMANS, GREEN, AND CO.

AND NEW YORK: 15 EAST 16th STREET.

1889.

PREFACE.

IT was originally intended that the two volumes of the 'Rotifera' should contain all the foreign, as well as all the British species; but, while the work was being written, so many new British forms were discovered, that want of space compelled the authors to omit all but a few of the more remarkable foreign Rotifera. The Supplement, however, now remedies this omission; and completes the work, by describing every known foreign species, as well as the British that have been discovered since its publication in 1886.

Upwards of one hundred and fifty species [1] have been added, in the Supplement, to the two hundred and fifty already described in vols. i. and ii.; and, in almost every case, the description is accompanied by a figure. Besides these, more than forty doubtful, or imperfectly described species, have been briefly discussed, and occasionally illustrated. Both the descriptions and drawings of the foreign species have been taken from the original memoirs in which they first appeared; the doubtful, or insufficiently described species, as well as the mere synonyms, being distinguished from the others by their position in each genus, and by the arrangement of the type.

The Bibliography has been considerably enlarged, and now exceeds two hundred memoirs, the greater part of which I have studied: all of them directly refer to the subject, and most of them are well worth the reading.

It is hardly necessary to add, that the labour of condensing such a mass of materials into a short Supplement has been great; especially when conflicting statements had to be weighed, and there was no opportunity of checking them by observations on the animals themselves; but I was anxious to complete the work, and

---

[1] Sixty of these are new British species discovered by Mr. Gosse.

specially anxious that my colleague's last discoveries should be placed where he himself wished to have them.

The natural pleasure, with which I see the observations and studies of thirty-five years thus brought to a successful conclusion, has been indeed marred by the sad loss of my deeply lamented friend. His great knowledge and experience, his keen powers of observation, his artistic skill, and his rare gift of description are known to all, and have made him *facile princeps* among the writers on the Rotifera; but it is only those who, like myself, were privileged to know him intimately, that are aware how much more he was than an enthusiastic naturalist. I shall never forget the hearty welcome (when I first met him) that the veteran gave to the comparatively unknown student, or the gracious kindness with which he subsequently placed at my disposal his beautiful unpublished drawings and his ample notes.

A happy chance had led our observations to differing parts of the same subject, and our united labours have produced, in consequence, the now completed work; but I shall ever count it a still happier chance, that gave me not only such a colleague, but also such a friend.

C. T. HUDSON.

CONTENTS

OF

THE SUPPLEMENT.

———◦◦◦———

SUPPLEMENT

TO

THE ROTIFERA:

OR

WHEEL-ANIMALCULES.

BY

C. T. HUDSON, LL.D. CANTAB., F.R.S.

All these things, I say, declared by Jason of Cyrene in five books, we will assay to abridge in one volume. We have been careful, that they that will read may have delight, and that they that are desirous to commit to memory may have ease, and that all, into whose hands it comes, may have profit; leaving to the author the exact handling of every particular, and labouring to follow the rules of an abridgement. For to stand upon every point, and to go over things at large, and to be curious in particulars, belongeth to the first author of the story; but to use brevity, and to avoid much labouring of the work, is to be granted to him that will make an abridgement.—Book ii. of the Maccabees.

We continually forget, that brutes have not the advantage of obtaining accurate ideas, by spoken or written language. We do not realise the immensity of their ignorance. That ignorance, in combination with perfect cerebral clearness (ignorance and mental clearness are quite compatible), and with inconceivably strong instincts, produces a creature whose mental states we can never accurately understand. The impossibility of knowing the real sensations of animals—and the sensations are the life—stands, like an inaccessible and immovable rock, right in the pathway of our studies.—P. G. HAMERTON, "Chapters on Animals."

> The earth may smile,
> And deck herself, each May, vain thing! with flowers,
> And seem forgetful of the cruelties
> Enacted on her ever-changing stage,
> Till every spot, upon the storied surface,
> Is rank with tragic memories.
> The earth may smile, I say,
> But, like a new-made widow's mirth, it shocks one.
>
> SIR ARTHUR HELPS, "Realmah.'

There is much slaughter in the world of brutes, but there is little slavery; and the killing is done with merciful rapidity, ending life whilst its pulses still beat in their energy, and preventing infirmity and age. The brute creation has its diseases, but on the whole it is astonishingly healthy. It is full of an amazing vitality. The more we study animals, the more evident it is that they live, for the most part, in a heaven of exuberant health. That gladness which we seek, how often vainly, in artificial stimulants, the brute finds in the free coursing of his own uncontaminated blood. Which of us has not envied the glee of his own dog?— P. G. HAMERTON, "Chapters on Animals."

'Tis a very excellent piece of work, madam lady; would 'twere done.— SHAKESPEARE, "The Taming of the Shrew."

SUPPLEMENT.

—◆—

FLOSCULARIADÆ.

Floscularia Millsii, *Kellicott* (180), (Pl. XXXII. fig. 1).

SP. CII. **Lobes** *five; of very great length; extremely slender, twig-like, without knobs; fringed with two opposite rows of cilia, not in whorls.*

This elegant and very curious creature was found, by Dr. Kellicott, in Black Creek, Ontario, U. S., on *Utricularia vulgaris*, in 1885. A description of a very similar Rotiferon was sent to me, in 1886, by Mr. Thomas Whitelegge of Sidney, N. S. W.

Dr. Kellicott says: "The delicate, sub-cylindrical, gelatinous sheaths, of *F. Millsii*, are frequently found occupying the fork made by branch or leaf; however, they are often found without this protection; the animal is usually solitary, but sometimes occurs in small groups of three or more. The peduncle is short, as in most Floscules; the posterior, attenuate, muscular part [foot] is relatively long, and terminates rather abruptly in the short, broadly ovate body. The capacious, hyaline mouth-funnel is but little broader at its free edge than below; the free border is set a very little obliquely. The rim of this bowl bears five extremely long, flexible, tentacle-like, trochal lobes, which are without the least knob-like enlargement at their extremities. These organs are very similar to those of *Stephanoceros Eichhornii*, except in the character and distribution of the cilia; in fact they are quite suggestive of the long, flexible tentacles of a polyzoon. The cilia on the lobes are distributed throughout the entire length, fine, longer towards the extremities, those at the ends nearly half as long as the lobes; they are arranged on the lateral borders of the tentacles, and stand straight out, almost reaching those of the adjacent lobes. When the long lobes are being pushed out of the sheath, they are held close together in a bundle; the very long cilia are then shaken out, as it appears, and a shimmer runs over them, very much like that seen on the long arms of *F. coronetta* and *F. cornuta*, when they are unfolded.

"It is not a sensitive species, and very readily displays its ciliary crown. The usual procession of Infusoria may be seen steadily moving down its throat, nor does it reject Algæ that may be drawn into the vortex. One, two, and sometimes three eggs may be seen in the tube at a time. I have not yet had an opportunity to observe them until they are hatched. This I very much regret, for it would undoubtedly shed light upon its generic affinities, and determine whether it is a *Floscularia* or a *Stephanoceros*."

The dimensions of a large individual are as follows: length from foot disc to body $\frac{1}{13}$ inch; of body $\frac{1}{16}$; of lobes $\frac{1}{5}$ inch; total length to top of extended lobes $\frac{1}{5}$ inch, but sometimes not exceeding $\frac{3}{10}$ inch.

Mr. Whitelegge describes his Rotiferon as so much resembling a *Stephanoceros*, that at first he thought that it was one. The differences between the two were, however, great. "The structure of the foot was new to me; it ended in a short immobile stalk, which is not affected when the animal retracts or extends; neither does it alter if the Rotiferon is detached. There are three ring-like protuberances at the end of the foot, just above the stalk, which generally remain unaltered when the animal extends itself.

The lobes are five in number, and the cilia are like those of *Floscularia*, while the lobes are like those of *Stephanoceros*, having the same incurved appearance towards the apex. Its size is about ¼ that of *Stephanoceros*." If Mr. Whitelegge's specimen was full grown, the Australian Rotiferon would be less than half the size of the largest American specimen ; but of course it is not fair to judge from a solitary example—as this was.

FLOSCULARIA (?) CHIMÆRA, Hudson, sp. nov. (Pl. XXXII, fig. 2).

SP. CH. **Corona** *a two lobed cup; the dorsal* **lobe** *much the larger, like an overhanging hood; the ventral slightly notched; the edge of the cup fringed with setæ.* **Foot** *with two toes. One dorsal* **eye**. *No* **tube**. *Free swimming.*

This strange creature was discovered by Mr. V. Gunson Thorpe, in water round a fountain in the Botanical Gardens at Brisbane. It was a solitary specimen. While its general resemblance to a Floscule is obvious, yet it possesses characters unknown in the rest of the genus, or indeed in the family of the *Flosculariadæ*. For, first, the **body** forms, with the foot, one continuous slender cone, terminated by two small toes ; instead of being a pear-shaped body, ending in a long, narrow, toe-less foot. Next, there is only one red **eye**, obviously situated on the dorsal surface of the hood ; instead of there being two minute, deeply-sunk, cervical eyes. Again, no Floscule has either a mastax or gastric glands ; but Mr. Thorpe's *chimæra* has two large gastric glands, and an obvious mastax. To all these points of difference must be added the habit of swimming freely ; and the result is as exasperating to classify, as it is delightful to contemplate.

Length. About ¼₀ inch. **Habitat.** Botanical Gardens, Brisbane (Thorpe).

LIMNIAS CORNUELLA, Rousselet (196), (Pl. XXXII. fig. 4).

SP. CH. *Four horny* **processes** *on the dorsal surface below the corona ; ventral* **antennæ** *very long, each equal in length to half the greatest width of the corona ;* **tube** *slightly tapering, generally curved (and sometimes twisted), ringed, translucent at the extremities.*

This very well marked species was discovered by Mr. Charles Rousselet,[1] in November 1888, attached to the rootlets of a plant (*Triæna bogotensis*) growing on the surface of a hot-house tank in the gardens of the Royal Botanic Society, in Regent's Park ; and I am indebted to Mr. Rousselet's courtesy for the living specimens from which my figures were drawn. The ventral **antennæ**, which are usually fully extended, would be long in any of the *Melicertadæ*, and therefore contrast strongly with the setigerous stumps and pimples of *annulatus*, and *ceratophylli*. The chin projects in an elegant trifid curve, and the **corona** has an unusually wide dorsal gap (fig. 4 *b*). The animal is fond of holding itself in its tube in an unusual position ; so that the plane of its corona is at right angles to the longer axis of the tube. This latter is transparent and corrugated, like that of *annulatus*, only the corrugations are broader and shallower ; and the tube itself is frequently obscured (especially in the middle) by fine granulations, and small brown, circular discs. Mr. Rousselet (*loc. cit.*) has given some excellent drawings of the tube (as well as of *cornuella* itself), showing its curved form, and the curious twist that it occasionally takes.

Length. From ₁⁄₂₅ to ¼₀ inch. **Habitat.** See above.

LIMNIAS GRANULOSUS, Weber (199).

SP. CH. **Corona** *formed of two great lobes, dorsal* [2] *cleft deep ; six* **processes** *on the dorsal surface, underneath the corona ; three* **antennæ**. **Tube** *cylindrical, opaque,*

---

[1] Mr. Thomas Whitelegge of Sydney, N.S.W., in a list of Rotifera which he had found in his neighbourhood in 1883-4, describes a *Limnias* in some respects similar to *cornuella*. He says : "Its tube is fusiform, opaque brown and often curved. The most marked characteristic is the length of the two antennæ, which project beyond the disc, when the cilia are in full play ; and also out of the tube, when the creature is retracted."

[2] There is some confusion here in the terms. If by the "dorsal cleft" above ("échancrure dorsale

yellow, strewed with round brown granules ; transversely striated on the inside ; foot forked.

M. Weber has drawn this *Limnias* with three antennæ all on the same surface[1] : one long, un-paired ; and the paired two, short. As such an arrangement is unknown in the *Melicertadæ*, I have not reproduced his figure ; especially as he himself states that all three are on the dorsal side. The foot, too, is described as "forked," and the foot-glands as discharging their secretion through an aperture in the angle of the fork. This structure and arrangement are unlike those in the foot of any other Floscule. The whole account requires confirmation.

Length. Not recorded. Habitat. Neighbourhood of Geneva (Weber).

LIMNIAS SHIAWASSEËNSIS, *Kellicott* (181).

SP. CII. *Seven horny* processes *on the dorsal surface below the corona ;* ventral antennæ *long, nearly equal to the diameter of the tube ;* tube *slightly increasing in breadth from below upwards, clear below, covered above by dark floccose, not smooth or annulate, but beset with transverse parallel rows of minute raised points.*

Dr. Kellicott found this apparently rare Rotiferon, in July 1888, on *Myriophyllum* in the Shiawassee river at Corunna, Michigan, U.S. It resembles *cornuella* in the length of its antennæ, but there are several points of difference in structure and habit between the two. "The coronal discs, when acting, are not pushed so far above the tube as in the other species—the lower edges just clearing the margin of the tube ; the discs are held nearly vertical, and the long ventral antennæ stand out considerably higher than the discs and at a sharp angle with the tube. The antennæ are slender, nearly straight, and terminated by a slender cone which bears a brush of setæ ; when the lobes are withdrawn, and the corona is just concealed, the antennæ stand up above the tube, and the extremity and brush of setæ are then seen to be invaginated. The corneous denticles [horny processes] are seven in number. In the middle line, just below the dorsal gap, there are two arising from a common base, their apices are obtuse. On each side of these, a little lower, is another with obtuse apex ; this pair points obliquely upward towards the uppermost pair. Below these, wider apart, are two more, broad and set obliquely ; and below this pair, near the middle line, is another pair, broad and set obliquely. The cloaca may be seen thrust up to the rim of the tube, between these processes, to discharge the fæces. The chin is obscurely lobed at its apex." (Kellicott, *loc. cit.*)

Length. Not recorded. Habitat. Shiawassee river, U. S. (Kellicott).

ŒCISTES SOCIALIS, *Weber* (199).

SP. CII. Body *elongated ;* corona *small, circular ;* foot, *twice as long as the body ;* teeth, *three ;* one *ventral* antenna ; *two* eyes *in the young.*

This *Œcistes* was discovered by M. Weber, in 1886, inhabiting a parasitic growth of

profonde ") is meant the deep V-shaped cleft on the oral surface, at the bottom of which the lobes meet, and the whole of whose edge is fringed with cilia, then the term "dorsal" is a mistake for "ventral" ; but if "échancrure" means the wide, non-ciliated, gap in the corona, between the lower portions of the two coronal lobes, then, though the term "dorsal" is correct, yet the attribute "profonde" is singularly inappropriate. Most probably the term "échancrure" stands for the V-shaped cleft on the oral surface, and for "dorsal cleft" we should read "ventral cleft."

[1] The text says that there are "two lateral tentacles," one on each side of the dorsal cleft ("échancrure dorsale"), and, "lower down dorsally, in the median line of the body is one long dorsal tentacle." An inspection of M. Weber's figure (Pl. xxvii. fig. 4), however, shows at a glance that the long, unpaired antenna is really meant to be on the same surface as the two, short, paired antennæ ; for it intercepts the view of the ventral (*i.e.* oral) surface on which the shortest pair are placed. Moreover, in the same figure, the lower portion of the coronal lobe, on the spectator's right hand, is curved backward *away* from him ; clearly proving that the surface he is looking at, and on which *all three* antennæ are placed, is the oral, or ventral one.

greenish-yellow, slightly gelatinous balls, on the stems of water plants. The ten or twenty individuals, of each group of this social Rotiferon, are all fixed towards the point which attaches the parasite to the plant. No distinct tubes are visible; but the Œcistes are immersed in a continuous mass similar to the tubes of other species of the genus.

The animal expands and contracts continually, and with great vivacity. Its great length, and its corona, place it close to Gosse's *serpentinus*, but it has not the dorsal hooks of this latter. M. Weber describes the **corona** as a circular single curve of cilia, notched slightly on the dorsal side, and fringing the edge of a deep funnel with a central buccal opening at the bottom of it. If this description be correct, then of course the animal is no *Œcistes*: nor can it belong to the *Melicertadœ* at all; for these have all laterally placed mouths, lying behind, and *outside of*, an imperforate disc, and on this disc are *two* parallel rows of cilia, the lower of which is continued round the buccal aperture. M. Weber adds that there are two obvious **salivary glands** above the mastax; **gastric glands; contractile vesicle** and **lateral canals**; and *one* short, setigerous, ventral **antenna.** He could not detect the **nervous ganglion**; but he says that, though he was prevented by the dark-coloured intestine and by the habitat of *socialis* from studying its internal structure thoroughly, yet he was satisfied that it had a strong similarity to other species of the same genus.

The unpaired **antenna**, which M. Weber describes as being on the ventral surface, is unlike anything in the *Melicertadœ*. But so short and wide apart are the paired ventral antennæ in *Œ. crystallinus*, that it is most difficult to get a view of both together; and it has been frequently asserted in consequence that it has but one. It is probable, therefore, that there are really *two* antennæ on the ventral surface of *socialis*.[1]

Length. Not recorded. **Habitat.** Near Geneva (Weber).

ŒCISTES MUCICOLA, *Kellicott* (181).

SP. CII. **Corona** *small, only slightly wider than the body, nearly circular;* **foot** *narrow, smooth, and, when fully extended, twice to thrice the length of the body; one minute horny* **process** *on the dorsal surface, just below the corona;* **ventral antennæ** *and* **tube** *apparently absent.*

"This interesting Rotiferon was found in abundance in a quiet pool, exposed to the sun, and in which great quantities of the gelatinous thalli of *Nostochacew* and *Rivulariacew* abounded. Little globules of the alga *Gloiotricha pisum* were attached to the dissected leaves of *Myriophyllum*, and in nearly all, one or more of the parasites were lodged, and in some, several found shelter. There is no apparent tube; the foot is usually attached near the centre of the small masses, and the disc pushed out beyond the surface. It is an exceedingly sensitive species, retiring to shelter at the least noise or shock. The body of the animal resembles somewhat that of *serpentinus*, but instead of two dorsal hooks below the corona there is one corneous tooth [**process**] not at all hooked; the foot is not thick when extended, nor wrinkled, but attenuate and smooth; its manners are not similar to those of *serpentinus*, as described by Mr. Gosse, and the eggs are of decidedly different shape and colour," being long-ovate and colourless. (Kellicott, *loc. cit.*)[2]

---

[1] I have not copied either of M. Weber's figures, as I think that there must be grave mistakes both in the description and in the drawings. It is most unlikely that the corona should have only one wreath of cilia, and that the usual imperforate disc should be converted into a deep funnel, with the mouth at the bottom of it.

[2] This may possibly be M. Weber's *Œ. socialis*, as they are alike in corona, foot, absence of tube, and in their parasitic habit. But M. Weber says that *socialis* has no dorsal hooks, and one ventral antenna; whereas Professor Kellicott could find no ventral antennæ, but saw one dorsal horny process.

Lacinularia pedunculata, *Hudson*, sp. nov.

The following account of this Australian species was sent to me by Mr. Thomas Whitelegge, who found it at Sydney, N. S. W, in 1886.

"This is a very remarkable form, and a cluster might easily be mistaken for a fallen flower of an acacia. The clusters are yellowish orange, a quarter of an inch in diameter, having a peduncle or stalk half an inch long, formed by the united feet of the animals. The union is so complete, that it was only after a great amount of patient investigation, that I became certain of the peduncle's consisting of many intertwined feet. The trochal disc seems to me to be intermediate in shape between that of *L. socialis*, and that of *Megalotrocha alboflavicans*. The gelatinous material, in which the animals are immersed, is well developed. This species I have found in abundance, after heavy rains, in shallow pools. Its period of activity is very brief, and the winter ova, as well as the ordinary ones, are soon formed in great numbers." [1]

Megalotrocha semi-bullata, *Hudson*, sp. nov. (Pl. XXXII. fig. 8).

SP. CH. **Corona** *four-sided;* opaque **warts** *two;* ventral **antennæ** *two small setigerous tubercles;* dorsal **antennæ** *apparently absent.*

Mr. Gunson Thorpe, who found this new *Megalotrocha* near Brisbane, describes it as forming free-swimming clusters of several Rotifera, adhering to one another by the tips of their feet, but without any tubes. The **corona** is not round, but four-sided; and the lower portion of the **foot** is distinctly marked out from the rest by three confluent swellings, where the upper portion joins it, one on each side, and one on the dorsal surface. Mr. Thorpe says that the animal contracts no further than the top of this trifid knob. The two opaque **warts** are on the ventral surface, one on each shoulder, and stand out prominently, above the surface of the body, when the ciliary wreath is withdrawn (fig. 8 *b*) : the two ventral antennæ lie just below the opaque warts, and the eyes are on the upper edge of the ciliary wreath, between the two rows of cilia (fig. 8 *a*), a most unusual position. The rest of the structure is normal. Mr. Thorpe has seen the **male**, which has a squarish corona like that of the female.[2]

Length, of an individual, $\frac{1}{50}$ inch. **Habitat.** Acclimatisation Gardens, Brisbane.

Philodina macrostyla, *Ehrenberg* (12), (Pl. XXXII. fig. 6).

SP. CH. **Body** *much fluted longitudinally; frontal* column *long, tapering;* antenna *with a small, three-lobed, club-shaped, terminal joint;* eyes *narrow, obliquely set;* teeth *three, thick;* spurs *long, slender, slightly sigmoid, acute.*

Ehrenberg's specific characters are "**Body** white, smooth ; **eyes** oblong ; **spurs** very long." But I have no doubt that this Rotifer is Mr. Gosse's *P. tuberculata*, the specific characters of which I now give to it. Each has a long, tapering, frontal **column** ; very long, narrow, sharp **spurs** ; a stout **antenna**, with hairs set on a trifid knob at the free end ; obliquely set, narrow **eyes** ; and three **teeth** in each ramus. Each, too, has a smooth white **skin** ; for, when *tuberculata* is put into clean water, it drops its floccose covering, and appears free from spine or tubercle.[3] The last joint of the foot divides

---

[1] I am indebted to Mr. Whitelegge for some specimens preserved in spirit. The long stalk is formed of intertwined mucous threads which issue from the extremity of the *Lacinulariæ* ; one pair of threads from each. This is obvious in the portion of the stalk which forms the diameter of the cluster ; but the ribbed appearance gradually fades away towards the lower end, where the mucous threads seem to have been fused together.

[2] In consequence of this discovery of Mr. Thorpe's, the characteristics of the Genus *Megalotrocha* (vol. i. p. 86) will require some alteration. Instead of " trunk with four opaque warts " read " trunk with opaque warts," and for " antennæ absent " read " antennæ absent or inconspicuous." The SP. CH. of *Megalotrocha alboflavicans* may now be given as follows : " Opaque warts four ; antennæ apparently absent."

[3] Mr. Gosse, in one of his last notes, says " *P. tuberculata* has no tubercles." Mr. G. Western, who

into two equal branches, each carrying a pair of unequal **toes** (fig. 6 *b*) ; the outer of which is the larger of the two. It is a fine handsome Rotifer, and not restless ; so that its structure can be easily observed.

Length, $\frac{1}{30}$ inch. **Habitat.** Neighbourhood of London (G. Western).

PHILODINA MICROPS, *Gosse* (171), (Pl. XXXI. fig. 1).

[SP. CH. **Body** *very slender, closely resembling* Rotifer vulgaris, *both in form and manners, but with eyes distinctly pectoral, small, round, of very pale red hue.* **Column** *thick, rounded, with minute hooked proboscis at front ;* **spurs** *rather small, separated by a horizontal edge ;* **corona** *in action not wider than head.*

This can scarcely be confounded with any recorded *Philodina.* For some time I felt sure it was *Rotifer vulgaris,* and marvelled that I could not see the eyes in the column. But when I looked to the *pectus,* they were plain enough, though very pale. I know no other species, whether of *Rotifer* or *Philodina,* with so very small a corona in rotation. The whole trunk is fluted. The viscera are tinged with pale smoke-brown, deepest in the abdominal canal. In some examples the hue is rather of a chestnut-brown.

I have examined perhaps half-a-dozen specimens, inhabiting the conferva of marine rock-pools in the Firth of Tay. The species is very shy of rotating, thus differing from other *Philodinæ,* which are characteristically free. At the moment of extruding the column, its broad extremity opens a central orifice which is strongly ciliated around its margin, while a row of cilia, apparently *few* and *distant,* is seen fringing the outer edge. The antenna consists of (two ?) telescopic joints, its dilated extremity carrying four divergent setæ.

Length, $\frac{1}{50}$ inch. **Habitat.** Firth of Tay. P. II. G.]

P. COLLARIS, *Ehrenberg* (12)=*P. erythrophthalma* (vol. i. p. 99).

P. SETIFERA, *Schmarda* (135), (Pl. XXXII. fig. 7), is said to have a row of setæ running down the foot, of which I give Schmarda's figure.

P. GRACILIS, P. CALCARATA, P. MACROSIPHO, *Schmarda* (134). See note below.[1]

ROTIFER TRISECATUS, *Weber* (199), (Pl. XXXII. fig. 9).

SP. CII. **Body** *a dull grey ;* **skin** *rough, with longitudinal and transverse folds, so as to form twelve apparent segments ; a coarse fold near the neck.* **Body** *elongated, cylindrical, diminishing suddenly ; truncated, at the level of the anus, to form a* **foot** *narrower than the rest of the body ;* **proboscis** *long ;* **eyes** *two ;* **coronal lobes** *short ;* **teeth** *two ;* **pharynx** *stout ;* **intestine** *generally coloured brown ;* **spurs** *movable at their extremity, long and slender ;* *three long, slender* **toes,** *divided into three segments.*

This Rotifer is rendered distinct from others, by the exaggerated length of its spurs and toes, and by the division of the latter into three joints, of which the last is capable of a feeble motion. The **corona** when expanded is scarcely wider than the neck ; the **proboscis** is stout, cylindrical, long, stretching much beyond the expanded corona, and seldom retracted even when the corona is in action. It bears two ovoid **eyes.** Unlike that of other species, the end of the **foot** is usually extended, showing the three toes.[2]

Length. About double that of *R. vulgaris.* **Habitat.** Near Geneva (Weber).

kindly sent me many living specimens, had noticed the same thing. Mr. D. Bryce, also, some time ago, forwarded to me a sketch of *tuberculata's* four toes.

[1] Both of Schmarda's pamphlets (134) and (135) contain species said to be new, but so drawn and described that it is not possible to do anything else than omit them.

[2] There is, in the description of the figures, a confusion of terms similar to that in *Limnias granulosus.* Fig. 2, Pl. xxx., in M. Weber's pamphlet, is said to represent the dorsal surface ; and the bent foot in it is said to be showing its ventral surface ; and yet that surface is the one that bears the spurs, and consequently is really the dorsal or anti-oral surface. To make it more perplexing, the proboscis seems, in the figure, to be on the opposite surface to the spurs.

ROTIFER ELONGATUS, *Weber* (199), (Pl. XXXII. fig. 8).

SP. CII. **Body** *greyish;* **cuticle** *crossed by transverse folds forming thirteen or fourteen segments; lobes of the* **corona** *small.* **Proboscis** *short;* **eyes** *two, round, red;* **teeth** *two;* **toes** *three, long, cylindrical, slightly apart, retractile.* **Spurs** *thick at the base, short, with mobile free extremities.*

The **corona** of *elongatus* is scarcely wider than the greatest breadth of the body, and the whole animal when extended forms a long, gently tapering, cone. The length of the fully extended **foot** is about ⅓ of the whole Rotifer. The corona is feeble, and the animal rarely swims, but creeps swiftly. The proboscis is short and thick, bearing an aureola of cilia. The foot has six segments, gradually diminishing in size from the cloaca to the toes. The spurs are widely divergent, slightly curved, and pointing somewhat to the toes: their tips are faintly articulated, and mobile. The three toes are long, round, and cylindrical, like little worms; and, once displayed, they separate slightly, in order to fix themselves on an object: they are usually retracted. M. Weber says that this species is distinguished from others of the genus by the form and length of the toes, which resemble the toes of *Actinurus*, with this difference, " that the toes [of *Actinurus*] are very long and *non-retractile*, remaining always extended, and acting somewhat as points of support (*un balancier*)." Here, however, M. Weber is in error. Both Mr. Gosse [1] and myself have often seen the toes of *Actinurus* drawn in, just like those of any other *Rotifer.*

Length. Almost that of *Actinurus neptunius.* **Habitat.** Near Geneva (Weber).

R. ERYTHRÆUS, *Ehrenberg* (42), is an imperfectly observed, and very doubtful species.
R. MAXIMUS, *Bartsch* (7),=*R. tardus* (vol. i. p. 105).
R. INFLATUS, *Dujardin* (40), is a species formed by confounding together several *Philodinæ*; and by refusing to distinguish between the genera *Philodina* and *Rotifer.*
R. MEGACEROS, *Schmarda* (184), (Pl. XXXII. fig. 10.) is said to have a pair of spurs on each of the last two joints of the foot; those on the penultimate joint being very long and curved: I have given Schmarda's figure of the spurs.

CALLIDINA PIGRA, *Gosse* (169), (Pl. XXXI. fig. 2).

[SP. CII. **Body** *fusiform, fluted, not collared;* **column** *having a decurved acute hook;* **spurs** *minute;* **viscera** *rufous.*

I have seen two examples, both of which had the extremities colourless, but the middle tinged of a delicate sherry-brown, the viscera somewhat deeper in hue; while in one was an immense egg, of a coffee-brown, almost opaque, whose appearance suggested the probability that the species is strictly oviparous. The acute hooked proboscis is very conspicuous. The corona, scarcely divided, is not wider than the neck at the antenna, and this neck is not swollen into a collar. The penultimate spurs are very minute cones, whose bases are not separated by an interspace. The whole central body is indented with longitudinal furrows. The **mallei** are destitute of visible teeth.

The animal is remarkably sluggish, rarely swimming, but turning its head slowly and aimlessly from side to side.

Length. When extended, $\frac{1}{50}$ inch. **Habitat.** Woolston Pond. P. H. G.]

CALLIDINA SYMBIOTICA, *Zelinka* (205), (Pl. XXXII. fig. 12).

SP. CII. **Body** *of sixteen segments, longitudinally furrowed, colour reddish, intestine a deeper yellowish-red;* **teeth** *two in one ramus and three in the other;* **œsophagus** *without a loop;* **corona** *large, with a short peduncle;* **upper lip** *notched, so as to have two little flaps;* **spurs** *short; two* **toes,** *each ending in five minute hollow prominences.*

---

[1] Mr. Gosse says: " These 'the toes' are often retracted in various degrees, even when the foot is otherwise extended."—*Evenings at the Microscope.* p. 300.

This *Callidina* was discovered by Dr. Carl Zelinka, inhabiting the *Jungermanniæ Frullania dilatata, F. tamarisci*, and *Radula complanata*. Dr. Zelinka has published an elaborate treatise on this form, explaining its structure most minutely, and accompanied by many large drawings and diagrams. The main differences, between it and the other species of the genus, are in the **mastax** and the **foot**. The first has rami with unequal numbers of teeth; and the second has toes, each of which ends in five small tubes, leading up to the foot-glands. Dr. Zelinka kindly sent me his treatise, and I at once went to some elms, on Clifton Down, on whose trunks I knew that the above-named plants were to be found. There was a bitter frost, and the snow lay deep; and though I procured plenty of the brown withered-looking *Frullania*, I had little hope of finding any Rotifera in its cups. However, on tearing out the brown mass with needles, I saw some green stems under the brown ones; and on moistening these under the microscope, I soon had the pleasure of seeing first one *Callidina*, and then another, come to life, stretch its head out of the cup in which it had been curled up, and unfurl its wheels (fig. 12 *a*). Dr. Zelinka describes the foot-glands (fig. 12 *b*) as consisting of four rows of cells, and their long excretory ducts as discharging through ten little tubes, five of which project from each toe. A somewhat similar arrangement has been discovered by Dr. Zelinka in *Discopus Synaptæ*, and I know of no other example among the *Philodinadæ*; but a mastax in which the rami have an unequal number of teeth is occasionally met with; individuals, of the same species, differing from each other in this respect. It is obvious how the *Callidina* contrives to exist in its strange home. Rain usually takes a definite course down the furrows in the bark of a tree, just as it does down the valleys of a river-basin; and the *Jungermanniæ* follow its track. The green cups are filled by the rain, and protected from rapid evaporation of their contents by the minuteness of their apertures, and their position on the under side of the frond. They thus form suitable homes for the *Callidina*; which, when at last the water begins to dry up, draws in its head and foot, shapes itself into a ball, exudes a gelatinous covering around itself, and waits for happier times.

Length, (fully extended) *cir.* ₁/₇, inch. **Habitat.** Cups and leaves of *Jungermanniæ*.

CALLIDINA LEITGEBII, *Zelinka* (205).

SP. CII. **Body** *of sixteen segments, longitudinally furrowed, colourless, alimentary canal generally full of green algæ;* **teeth** *in one ramus five, in the other six;* **œsophagus** *with a loop;* **corona** *large, with a short peduncle;* **upper lip** *not notched, but with a median projection;* **spurs** *short; two toes, each ending in five minute hollow prominences.*

A very similar animal to the last; and also found by Dr. Zelinka in *Jungermanniæ*. It is said to have the same peculiar toes.

Length, *cir.* ₁/₃₀ inch. **Habitat.** Cups and leaves of *Jungermanniæ* (Zelinka).

CALLIDINA QUADRICORNIFERA, *Milne.*

Macrotrachela quadricornifera . . . . . . Milne (186).

SP. CII. **Body** *stout, and Philodine-like;* **corona** *large, not constricted;* **proboscis** *very thick and square;* **foot** *about ⅓ of total length, and with three short thick toes;* **spurs** *four, there being an extra pair on the top joint of the foot.*

This species of Mr. Milne's is remarkable for the extra pair of spurs on the foot. The general shape is not unlike that of *P. citrina*, and the wheels are very similar; but the **foot** is much shorter in proportion. The **mastax** is large, and so is the **contractile vesicle**. There is a short, broad, perforate **antenna**, armed with fine setæ; and the transverse **muscular system** is well developed.

Length, ₁/₇₀ inch. **Habitat.** Neighbourhood of Glasgow (Milne).

CALLIDINA ACULEATA, *Milne* (Pl. XXXII. fig. 11).

Macrotrachela aculeata . . . . Milne (186).

SP. CII.   **Body** *somewhat fish-shaped, with three or four posterior rows of spines, and one anterior row near the mastax;* **foot** *about ¼ of total length, with three short toes;* **spurs** *¾ width of penultimate joint.*

Mr. Milne met with but few specimens of this remarkable *Callidina*. Its body has many longitudinal furrows; and Mr. Milne draws the four rows of **spines** with as many as five or six spines in each row.

Length, ₁₀₀¹ inch.   **Habitat.**   Near Glasgow (Milne).

CALLIDINA SOCIALIS, *Kellicott* (181).

SP. CII.   **Corona** *relatively wide;* **column** *thick and ciliated;* **dorsal antenna** *short, terminated by many minute, setiferous pointed elevations;* **spurs** *long and stout;* **teeth** *two.*   **Parasitic** *on the limbs and dorsal folds of the larva of the beetle* Psephenus Lecontei.

It is a slender elongate form; when the body is fully extended the width of the **corona** considerably exceeds that of the body.   The **body** is transparent, without colour, except the light brown of the stomach, apparently imparted by contents of that hue.   The longitudinal flutings of the trunk, and the transverse folds above and below these are conspicuous.   The **contractile vesicle** was not observed.   Many examples of the larva were examined, every one of which was infested by the Rotiferon; often scores were witnessed, clinging in groups.

Length, (when fully extended) ₅⁴ inch.   **Habitat,** Corunna, Michigan (Kellicott).

CALLIDINA CONSTRICTA, *Dujardin* (40).—Dujardin merely states that this *Callidina* has a very small corona, and rami crossed by fine parallel teeth.   There is neither description nor figure of the proboscis, dorsal antenna, or foot; it is impossible to say whether it is distinct from those species already described.

CALLIDINA CORNUTA, *Perty* (124).—This also is an imperfectly described animal.   Perty only says that it is neither *constricta* nor *elegans,* that it has a *Notommata*-like projection on each side of the head, and that its jaws are like those of *constricta.*   He gives no figure.

CALLIDINA REDIVIVA, *Ehrenberg,* is described as being " fusiform, diffusely granular, or else fleshy; with red distinct ova, and strong rotatory organs.   In the sediments of water-spouts of houses, Berlin.   Length, ₁₀¹ to ₄¹ inch." [1]

C. ALPINA and C. SCARLATINA, *Ehrenberg,* are Alpine species, of which I can find no details; except that *scarlatina* was found dried up, like pink dust, near the tops of the Alps.

Genus DISCOPUS, *Zelinka* (206).

GEN. CH.   *One of the Philodinadæ;* **eyeless,** *the last two joints of the* **foot** *converted into a great sucker;* *the* **foot glands** *arranged in two transverse rows, and fastened laterally and ventrally to the inner surface of the body-wall;* **ducts** *of the foot glands running down to the last joint of the foot, and insulated in a capsule.*

DISCOPUS SYNAPTÆ, *Zelinka* (206), (Pl. XXXII. fig. 5).

This parasitical Rotiferon was discovered by Professor E. Ray Lankester, in 1868, in the body-cavity of the *Synapta* of the Channel Islands.   Dr. Lankester had neither the

[1] Pritchard's *Infusoria,* 4th ed. p. 702.

time, nor the opportunity, to invesiigate its structure thoroughly ; but he gave two characteristic sketches of the ventral and lateral surfaces, showing the remarkable sucking disc
in the foot. According to Dr. Carl Zelinka, who has since found it on the surface of
the Channel *Synaptæ*, the corona is short, but slightly expanded ; there are ciliated
cushions on each side of the buccal aperture, and this latter widens at the top into a
projecting beak. The internal structure resembles that of *Callidina*, except that there
is no **contractile vesicle**. The **lateral canals** and vibratile tags, though present, are
hard to find. The penultimate joint of the **foot** (figs. 5 *a*, 5 *b*) has been altered into a
circular sucking disc placed ventrally, and bearing in its centre a circular raised collar
or cup, into which the ducts of the foot-glands open. This cup may be considered to be
the altered last joint of the foot. There are twelve completely separated **gastric glands**,
arranged in two rows, one above another, round the lower ventral portion of the trunk.[1]

Length, ₁|ₙ to about ₁|₁₅ inch (Zelinka) ; ₇⁵₀₀ inch (Lankester). **Habitat**. Parasi-
tical on the skin, and in the body-cavity, of *Synaptæ*.

ADINETA OCULATA, *Milne.*

Callidina oculata .   .   .   .   Milne (186).

SP. CII. **Body** *spindle-shaped ;* **head** *small ;* **mastax** *and rami very small, the latter
with two transverse teeth each ;* **spurs** *the width of the penultimate joint ;* **toes** *three, half
the length of the spurs ;* **eyes** *two, large, brilliant red.*

Mr. Milne's species is a stouter animal than *vaga*, and can at once be distinguished
from it by its pair of brilliant red **eyes**. It has also a pair of obvious **gastric glands** ;
whereas in *vaga* they are either inconspicuous, or absent.

Length, ₃|₆ inch. **Habitat**. Near Glasgow (Milne).

ASPLANCHNA SIEBOLDII, *Leydig* (110), (Pl. XXXII. fig. 14).

Dr. Leydig, who discovered this *Asplanchna* in 1853, says (*loc. cit.*) that the female
so closely resembles *A. Brightwellii*, that he should have considered them identical, had
it not been for the difference in shape between the males. As Dr. Leydig has observed
the male in the ovi-sac, there is no room for suggesting that the male of one species
might have been accidentally captured among the females of another.

The male (fig. 14), like that of *A. Ebbesbornii*, has two cervical **humps** and two
lateral ; but is sharply conical, the corona being the base of the cone, and the extremity
of the penis-sheath the apex. Its internal structure is well shown in Dr. Leydig's figure ;
and follows so exactly the plan of the male of *Ebbesbornii*, that further description is
unnecessary. Oddly enough, too, the markings on the ephippial egg of *Sieboldii* resemble
those on the ephippial egg of *Ebbesbornii*, and not of *Brightwellii*.

Length. Not recorded. **Habitat**. Dirty roadside ditch at Zell (Leydig).

ASPLANCHNA INTERMEDIA, *Hudson* (Pl. XXXII. fig. 15).

SP. CII. *The* **female** *indistinguishable from* A. Brightwellii : *the* **male** *with two
side* **humps,** *but none on the neck ; in other respects closely resembling the male of* A.
Brightwellii.

I found this *Asplanchna* in 1875, and described it, and its male, in the *Mon. Mic. J.*
of that year, p. 52, giving a sketch of the male. Of the female it is not necessary to
say more than that Mr. Gosse, who has studied it, agrees with me in saying that he
could not distinguish it from *Brightwellii*. The **contractile vesicle** and **sperm-sac** of

---

[1] Dr. Carl Zelinka's memoir on this parasitic Rotiferon gives the most minute description of its
whole structure, and is accompanied by a profusion of highly interesting figures. The whole memoir
deserves attentive study, containing, as it does, not only an exhaustive account of *Discopus synaptæ*,
but also full discussion of many topics concerning the Rotifera.

the male are very small; and the lateral canals have the vibratile tags arranged in a straight line on either side. The creature is so wonderfully transparent and empty, that it is difficult to see it even with a hand-lens, although $\frac{1}{6}$ inch in length. The hind dorsal corner of the body is somewhat prolonged into a sort of third hump, and darts out stiff and obvious (as do the lateral arms) when the head is retracted. The opposite ventral corner is prolonged, to a blunt point, and is the sheath of a long protusile penis. In one specimen I saw tags in which no ciliary motion was visible. What appears to be an atrophied œsophagus and stomach hangs freely in the body-cavity, between the head and the above-named dorsal hump. Mr. Gosse has seen the male *in utero*.

Length (male), $\frac{1}{60}$ inch. **Habitat.** Birmingham (P.H.G., and T.B.): Clifton (C.T.H.).

ASPLANCHNA AMPHORA, *Hudson*, sp. nov.

SP. CII. **Body,** *of female, conical, with one dorsal, and two lateral* **humps; eye** *single ;* **rami** *with long curved simply pointed ends, and a stout hook at the middle of the inner edge of each, not serrated ;* **contractile vesicle** *not large, expanding to very much less than half the body-cavity ;* **vibratile tags** *above forty on each side, and arranged in straight lines ;* **ovary** *a narrow ribbon ;* **male** *with two lateral humps.*

Professor Leidy kindly sent me this *Asplanchna*, in 1887, preserved in spirit; and I am indebted to Mr. G. Western for many living specimens. The female closely resembles *Ebbesbornii*; but the posterior extremity is almost conical, whereas in *Ebbesbornii* it is ventrally prolonged into a blunt curved hump. The two lateral humps, also, are nearer the middle of the body, and the ephippial **egg** is covered with dotted scales. Mr. Rousselet lately called my attention to the fact that the vibratile tags are crowned with a row of fine hairs, with a long one at each corner. Mr. G. Western has seen the male *in utero*.

Length, $\frac{1}{20}$ inch. **Habitat.** Philadelphia (Leidy); near London (Western).

ASPLANCHNA TRIOPHTHALMA, *Daday* (207).

SP. CII. **Female** *humpless ;* **head** *truncate ;* **eyes** *three—two smaller a little below the dorsal margin, one greater cervical ;* **vascular system,** *as in* priodonta ; **ovary,** *a transverse ribbon.* **Male** *humpless.*

Dr. Daday courteously sent me his memoir on this *Asplanchna*, which he found " in the great pool near Mezö-Záh." It distinctly differs from *priodonta* in the position of the two smaller eyes, and in the truncate head. Dr. Daday has given a drawing of the vibratile tags showing each crowned with a row of fine hairs.

Length. About $\frac{1}{12}$ inch. **Habitat.** See above (Daday).

A. HELVETICA, *Imhof* (179). I can see no difference between *helvetica* and *priodonta* ; but M. de Guerne (173) separates them, because *helvetica* has only six " denticulations " on the inner margin of each ramus, and its supplementary tooth, or uncus, is " strongly arcuate " ; while " the figures and descriptions " of *priodonta* give it more than six denticulations, and a " scarcely arcuate " uncus. I have examined many specimens of *priodonta*, since my attention has been called to these points, and I have always found six denticulations in each ramus (Pl. XXXIII. fig. 2) ; and that the apparent curvature of the uncus varies much with pressure, with the point of view, and with the individual. The wide dispersion of *helvetica* throughout Switzerland, Northern Italy, Austria, North and South Germany, Auvergne, Russian Lapland &c. &c., makes it highly probable that the two species are identical.

A. Herricki, *de Guerne* (173, 175), (Pl. XXXIII. fig. 5). SP. CII. " **Body** *amphora-shaped : trophi stout, consisting only of two rami, with an almost straight internal margin, terminated by a strong hook, with an apex not internally denticulated.*" Mr. Herrick, who discovered this *Asplanchna* in Minnesota, U. S., says it resembles *Bright-wellii* and is hermaphrodite. M. de Guerne (*loc. cit.*), while very properly discrediting the latter statement, forms a new species of it solely on account of the shape of the rami. As these, however, are of extraordinary shape and proportions, and have no fulcrum or unci, I think it better to wait till there is some further account of the creature published.

A. Girodi, *de Guerne* (173), (Pl. XXXIII. fig. 6). SP. CII. " **Body** *globose ; trophi elongated, stout, consisting only of two rami, each with a bidentate apex, having one tooth curved and sub-obtuse, the other compressed and lamellar.*" M. de Guerne says these trophi are distinguished from all others by the lamellar teeth just below the apex. But this is an error, for *Brightwellii, priodonta,* and *Ebbesbornii* have all these apparent lamellar teeth. In fact their rami, seen side-wise (Pl. XXXIII. fig. 2 *b*), are evidently deep plates bounded at the top by a thick broad ridge ; which, at the apex, is prolonged, beyond the plate, into a curved hook. When the ramus is subjected to pressure from above, the deep plate is bent by the glass (to which it stands at right angles), and its free lower corner is twisted, so as to look sometimes like a second tooth, just below the extreme apex, sometimes like a small plate : and often it is hidden altogether, under the thick curved pincer-like ridge, which alone is usually drawn as the ramus. I was unaware of this construction, till my attention was drawn to it by exactly reproducing M. de Guerne's figure of the trophi of *Girodi,* on crushing the trophi of *Brightwellii.* These latter are correctly drawn in fig. 4, Pl. XXXIII. Nor is this all. The unci dis-appeared entirely, as they have in the figure of *Girodi,* fig. 6, and the lines *a, a,* seen in that figure were shown to be the crushed remains of fibres (*b, b,* fig. 4), of the true nature of which I am in doubt.

There may be other characters which entitle *Girodi* to specific rank ; but the above are evidently insufficient.

A. Imhofi, *de Guerne* (173), (Pl. XXXIII. fig. 7). SP. CH. " **Body** *ovately globose ; trophi elongated, strong, composed only of two rami ; apex slightly incurved, bifid ;* **ramus** *armed, in the middle, with a stout internal tooth ;* **base** *of the ramus triangular, solid, with an external hook above.*" Here again the characters are taken almost solely from the trophi ; which are said, like those of *Girodi, Herricki,* and *Krameri,* to have no unci : no other part of the structure is described, and neither the male, nor the ephip-pial egg has been observed. Moreover there is an ambiguity in M. de Guerne's description and drawing. What is meant by the " solid, triangular bases of the rami " ? They seem, according to fig. 7, to be bounded by the lines *c, c* ; which are of the same depth of tint as the outer edges of the rami, and are continuous with them. But these lines are really the boundaries of a soft muscular mass which embraces the narrow ful-crum, *f.* The true bases of the rami are the curved lines, *d, d.* The same ambiguity exists in the drawing of *Girodi,* fig. 6. That these sloping lines, *c, c,* are the edges of muscle, and not of the hard parts of the jaws, is certain : for I have seen the fulcrum, *f,* moved slowly to and fro, like a pendulum, by the alternate contraction and expansion of the muscle on either side.

A. Imhofi may very possibly be a new species ; but the rami, as drawn in M. de Guerne's figure, are hardly enough to make it certain.

A. Krameri, *de Guerne* (173), (Pl. XXXIII. fig. 3). SP. CH. " **Body** *globose :* **trophi** *consisting only of two rami, which are curved, slender at the base, stout at the extremity, sickle-shaped, and with the interior margin denticulated.*" It will be seen that here the trophi, on which alone the creature's distinct specific rank is made to depend, have two fulcra ; one to each ramus. If the drawing be correct, then, the thin deep plate, of which the fulcrum consists, must have been split by violence evenly down its whole length—a rather unlikely thing. The unci, too, have been destroyed. Dr. Kramer's figure of *Krameri* shows an *Asplanchna* whose ovary, contractile vesicle, and lateral canals are those of *priodonta*. The drawing of the head teaches us nothing ; for it is represented merely as a puckered bag. Neither does the text help us much : for Dr. Kramer describes the oviduct as two fine threads, and the nerve-threads and rocket heads, of the ventral antennæ, as fine canals ending in oval bladders &c. &c. ; and he then unites the ventral antennæ, their nerve threads, the contractile vesicle, and the oviduct into one " Organ-komplex," which he says he cannot undertake to explain. It is impossible to say whether *A. Krameri* is a new species, or not.

For the reasons detailed above, I do not consider these four species as established ; but I ought to add that M. de Guerne's memoir on the *Asplanchnadæ*, in which they are found, is most interesting and suggestive, and contains very instructive details of the distribution of these charming Rotifera.

A. MAGNIFICA, *Herrick* (175) ; probably = *A. myrmeleo.*

Genus, ASPLANCHNOPUS, *de Guerne* (173).

GEN. CII. *An Asplancha with a ventral retractile foot, ending in two* **toes.**
This new genus we owe to M. de Guerne (*loc. cit.*), who has very properly separated the Rotifera it contains from the genus *Asplanchna*, on account of their possessing a foot.

ASPLANCHNOPUS MYRMELEO, *Ehrenberg* (Pl. XXXII. fig. 13).

Notommata myrmeleo   .   .   .   .   .   Ehrenberg (42).

SP. CII. **Female** *with short, wholly retractile* **foot,** *but without* **humps;** *eye single ;* **rami** *greatly curved, with simple pointed ends, not serrated ;* **contractile vesicle** *expanding to about half the body-cavity ;* **vibratile tags** *about fifty on each side, set on a separate, and very narrow, lateral canal ;* **ovary** *horse-shoe shaped, with broad and double, rounded ends.*

This handsome Rotiferon has only lately been found in Great Britain. Mr. Hood found it near Dundee in 1886, and sent it to Mr. Gosse, too late, unfortunately, for its insertion in the " Rotifera." It the summer of 1888, however, Mr. C. Rousselet kindly forwarded several specimens to me from Staines, all of which were female. It is an *Asplanchna* with a forked foot ; and the only points of its structure, that require notice, are the foot, the trophi, the gastric glands and the ovary. The **foot** is very short, ending in two minute toes, and springs from the ventral surface, into which it can be withdrawn by four muscles. The **trophi** are bent almost into a circle ; they are very massive at the base, but taper to fine points without any hooks, or serrations, to break their circular outline : neither did I notice any unci, such as are to be seen in *priodonta* and *Bright-wellii*. The **gastric glands** are so deeply bilobed, that the animal seems to possess four gastric glands, just like *Copeus spicatus*. The **ovary** is most remarkable, not only for its great size and peculiar shape (which will be best understood from the figure) but also from its being constantly thrown into ever varying curves ; now stretching the whole length of the body, and now drawn down into wavy folds towards the hinder end.

Mr. Geo. Western has described and figured [1] a male Rotiferon (Pl. XXXII. fig. 13 *b*) born in a trough filled with water obtained at Staines, where the female *A. myrmeleo* was then abundant. It is very probably the male of *myrmeleo* whose general appearance it much resembles ; especially in the characteristic **foot.** It has a large tripartite **brain,** and **eye spot**; two dorsal **antennæ**; a very large **contractile vesicle,** and numerous

[1] Mr. C. Rousselet described and drew the female, in the August number of *Science Gossip*, 1888. This led Mr. G. Western to hunt for the male, which he described and drew in the November number of the same year.

vibratile tags. There are the usual **sperm-sac** and protusile penis, the latter lying "behind the foot under a valve-like flap."

Length, of female, cir. $\frac{1}{35}$ in.; of male, cir. $\frac{1}{50}$ in. **Habitat.** Dundee (J. H.) ; Staines (Rousselet and Western).

ASPLANCHNOPUS SYRINX, *Ehrenberg* (Pl. XXXIV. fig. 37).

Notommata syrinx . . . Ehrenberg (42); Schmarda (134 and 135).

SP. CH. **Body** *bell-shaped ;* **foot** *very small, scarcely visible ;* **jaws** *(rami) curved, bifid at the point.*

This Rotiferon, according to Ehrenberg, is very similar to *A. myrmeleo*, but differs from it in the following points. The surface of the head is hardly visible, and has two minute toes ; the points of the **rami** are bifid ; and the **vibratile tags** are not more than from eight to thirteen on each side.

Schmarda found this Rotiferon in Egypt, and in a well on Adam's Peak in Ceylon. He noticed in one fœtus a secondary tooth to each ramus. No other observer appears to have met with this animal, except Weisse.

Length. About $\frac{1}{45}$ inch. **Habitat.** Berlin (Ehr.) ; Egypt and Ceylon (Schmarda) ; St. Petersburg (Weisse).

ASPLANCHNOPUS EUPODA, *Gosse* (Pl. XXXI. fig. 3).

Asplanchna eupoda . . . Gosse (169).

[SP. CII. **Body** *globose, with a stout foot, retractile at will ;* **rami** *of incus long, each armed on its inner edge with four widely-severed teeth.*

The most remarkable feature is the foot, which is, proportionally, much larger than in *A. myrmeleo*. The pincer-like rami are those of a normal *Asplanchna*, having a close resemblance to those of *A. priodonta*, save that their inner edges are not cut into saw-teeth, but beset with three distant spinous teeth, while each curved point is double. I have examined eight or ten examples, all from the canal, Smallheath, Birmingham.

Length, $\frac{1}{12}$ inch. **Habitat.** See above ; lacustrine. P.H.G.]

SACCULUS SALTANS, *Bartsch* (Pl. XXXII. fig. 24).

Ascomorpha saltans . . . . Bartsch (7, 8).

SP. CII. **Body** *with two dorsal longitudinal ridges, and two lateral ;* **lateral view** *sac-like, nearly symmetrical ;* **head** *truncate, with a lip-shaped projecting* **process** *on the mid-dorsal edge of its base ;* **corona** *a simple marginal circle.*

The **body** of *saltans* is bounded (says Dr. Bartsch) by four surfaces which meet in four longitudinal ridges, two dorsal and two lateral. Unlike *viridis*, its lateral view shows a dorsal outline very similar to the ventral ; and its flat head, with the thumb-like dorsal process, is very different from the low cone which rises from the neck of Mr. Gosse's Rotiferon. Its manners, too, are striking. Dr. Bartsch describes it as now hovering over the same spot, now suddenly darting forward, now turning on its longer axis, and now spinning round its transverse horizontal or vertical one ; and, when these antics are over, again returning to hover over the old spot as before.

Length, $\frac{1}{160}$ inch. **Habitat.** Near Tübingen (Bartsch).

SACCULUS HYALINUS, *Kellicott* (181), (Pl. XXXII. fig. 23).

SP. CII. **Body** *hyaline, with two lateral, sub-dorsal grooves ;* **lateral view** *oval, almost symmetrical, the dorsal outline a little more curved than the ventral ;* **dorsal view** *sac-like ;* **head** *depressed with a thin, downwards pointing, projecting process on its mid-dorsal edge ;* **corona** *a simple, marginal circle.*

" This ' bonnie gem ' was discovered among *Utricularia* and *Lemna* in a small pond shaded by alders and swamp-maples. The animal is an ovoid, hyaline sac, constricted anteriorly to a short cylindrical neck, which, when the corona is retracted, is fluted, and the free edge is crenate. There is on each side a sub-dorsal **groove**. The **corona** has a circlet of ample cilia, and at the dorsal border there is a conspicuous spatula-shaped **apex**, which, seen laterally, is thin and turned downwards; on each side of this is what appears to be a stout incurved seta. The **stomach** is large and lobed, of a rich yellowish brown. The **mastax** is an oblong clear globule, the apex of which is pushed to the front ; the trophi appear to be virgate. There is a large nearly globular **contractile vesicle**, which is situated near the posterior wall ; as it collapses, the extremity of the sac caves in, and occupies in part the space it filled. The large red **eye** is circular (fig. 23 *b*) seen dorsally, and concavo-convex seen obliquely from below. Dorsally viewed there is a brilliant circular centre, particularly when illuminated from the mirror below ; seen laterally there is disclosed a clear sphere (fig. 23 *c*) in the centre of the concave lower face : this seems to act like a lens."

Length, $_2\frac{1}{16}$ inch; width, $_3\frac{1}{16}$ inch. **Habitat.** Corunna, Michigan (Kellicott).

SACCULUS GERMANICUS, *Leydig* (Pl. XXXII. fig. 25).

Ascomorpha germanica . . . Leydig (110).

SP. CII. **Dorsal view** *sac-like ;* **head** *conical, with a triangular projecting process on the mid-dorsal edge of its base ;* **corona** *a simple marginal wreath, with several long styles set at intervals.*

It is with some hesitation that I give these specific characters taken from Leydig's description and figures. He himself notices three points of difference between *germanicus* and *Ascomorpha helvetica* (*S. viridis*), viz. that its coronal head is orange yellow, that its size is half that of *viridis*, and that its motions are peculiar—very similar, indeed, to those of *saltans*. His figure shows another peculiarity, namely the projecting of the back in a sort of triangular beak. He adds that he had seen as many as six round eggs (evidently male eggs) attached to one individual ; but that those, which carried the rough ephippial eggs, never had more than one at a time.

Length, $_3\frac{1}{100}$ inch.

The SP. CH. for SACCULUS VIRIDIS have not yet been given (vol. i. p. 124), as it was described as the solitary species of the genus. They are as follows :—

Dorsal view *sac-like ;* **ventral view** *unsymmetrical with a gibbous dorsal outline ;* **head** *conical, without a mid-dorsal process on the edge of its base ;* **corona** *a simple marginal circle, with several long styles set at intervals.*

SYNCHÆTA LONGIPES, *Gosse* (169), (Pl. XXXI. fig. 4 [1]).

[SP. CH. *In front much like* S. pectinata, *but with the foot distinct, separated, long, furnished with two small toes.*

The well-marked **foot**, having a rhomboid outline, common to all the eight or ten specimens that I examined, appeared to me sufficient, when combined with its small dimensions, to distinguish this species from *S. pectinata*, with which else it has much in common. The broad head bears four frontal warts and two setæ. It has occurred in some profusion in fresh water near Dundee. A great, occipital **brain** carries a well-defined eye, which appears black. The **foot** is capable of retraction as far as its angle, and is occasionally twitched up and vibrated.

Length, $_1\frac{1}{75}$ inch. **Habitat.** Fresh-water, Dundee. P.H.G.]

¹ Mr. Hood (177) says that Mr. Gosse's figure has been taken from a young animal.

S. GYRINA, *Hood* (176). This marine Rotiferon was found in spring time by Mr. Hood in a tide-pool in the estuary of the Tay along with *Mytilia tavina, Notholca spinifera,* and *Distemma raptor.* It disappeared throughout the summer and winter months, but reappeared in abundance in the following spring. It is so like *Synchœta baltica* that I hesitate to give it specific rank. The following are the points of difference which appear to separate the two in some degree. The **body** in Mr. Hood's drawing is narrower, just below the auricles, than it is further down; and from there it swells out till the middle of the animal is reached, from which point it again diminishes, and then suddenly lessens to form a base to the true foot. Both Ehrenberg and Mr. Gosse draw *S. baltica* as much more conical, and as gradually tapering to the foot. Mr. Hood says that it does not carry its eggs, as *baltica* does, but lays them at the bottom of the pool, on confervæ &c. Its mode of swimming is peculiar; for it swims always in circles: sometimes in wide ones, sometimes in circles not much exceeding its own length in their diameter, and it never swims head over heels, as *baltica,* cr *pectinata,* does.

The **male** is very slender, not over $\frac{1}{300}$ inch in length; with a broad corona and a pair of conspicuous red eyes. Mr. Hood observed the connection of the sexes, which took place while the female was in rapid motion, and lasted more than one minute; he also observed that the males had connection with young females only, never with the full grown.

Length, (of female) $\frac{1}{70}$ inch. **Habitat.** Tide pools, estuary of the Tay (J.H.).

POLYARTHRA HEXAPTERA, *Schmarda* (135). Schmarda found this Rotiferon in the great clay vessels of drinking water at Paita and Guyaquil. He says that on each side of the body three bristle-shaped spines spring from a common base; and that there are three teeth in each "maxilla." His figure (in other respects worthless) shows spines very similar to those in Ehrenberg's figure of *trigla* (see vol. ii. p. 3, note); so possibly there may be a *Polyarthra* with spines like those of a *Triarthra*: but his statement that there are three teeth in each "maxilla" is incomprehensible; unless (which is highly improbable) the trophi of his *Polyarthra* are on a different plan from those of *platyptera.*

Length. About $\frac{1}{250}$ inch.

TRIARTHRA TERMINALIS, *Plate* (126).

SP. CII. *Base of the unpaired* **spine**, *at the posterior extremity of the body; the spine itself almost immovable, and lying in a line with the ventral surface.*

Dr. Plate (*loc. cit.*) says that *terminalis* resembles *longiseta* in many respects, but differs from it in having the lowest of its three spines seated at the hinder end of the body, so that its base projects even beyond the orifice of the cloaca. Moreover, this spine does not move with the front pair, but generally remains extended in a line with the ventral surface. The length of the spines is variable, but Dr. Plate found that in many examples the length of the front pair was thrice that of the body; of the unpaired spine, twice: all three were usually free from imbrications, whereas those of *longiseta* are imbricated.

Length, $\frac{1}{130}$ inch. **Habitat.** Bonn (Plate).

T. CORNUTA, *Weisse* (126) = *T. breviseta.*

HYDATINA BRACHYDACTYLA, *Ehrenberg* (42). SP. CII. "**Body** *suddenly diminished at the base of the foot;* **toes** *minute.*" A very doubtful species. It was only $\frac{1}{17}$ inch in length, and was probably not adult. Ehrenberg's drawing adds nothing to his description.

H. CHILENSIS, *Schmarda* (135). The points of difference said to exist between this and *H. senta,* are that there are five teeth in each uncus, that the toes are longer, and that the gastric glands are pear-shaped. But gastric glands often differ in shape, and so occasionally does the number of teeth in an uncus. At the most, *chilensis* may be a variety; it is $\frac{1}{25}$ inch long, and was found in St. Jago, Chili.

H. TETRAODON, and H. MACROGNATHA, *Schmarda* (135). See note 1, Sup^t, p. 8.

Genus TRIPHYLUS, *Hudson*.

GEN. CH. *A genus of the* NOTOMMATADÆ; *body sub-cylindrical, somewhat compressed, gibbous dorsally; foot short, retractile, on the ventral surface; eyes two, frontal.*

TRIPHYLUS LACUSTRIS, *Ehrenberg* (Pl. XXXII. fig. 16).
Diglena lacustris . . . . . Ehrenberg (42).

SP. CH. **Corona** *without setigerous prominences;* **ciliary wreath** *single;* **foot** *about one-fifth of the total length;* **trophi** *forcipate;* **skin** *slightly thickened into two ridges on the dorsal surface.*

No one appears to have studied this Rotiferon since Ehrenberg described it; so it was with great pleasure that I examined some living specimens, kindly sent to me by Mr. George Western, who had found them in a pond at Littleton.

The animal closely resembles *Notops clavulatus* in the greater part of its internal structure, and *Notops hyptopus* in its general shape; while it differs from both in having two frontal eyes, and no solitary cervical one. It is quite unlike the *Diglenæ*; among which it was placed solely on account of its two frontal eyes. The **body** is sac-like; not nearly so compressed as that of *hyptopus*; the head, transversely truncate and slightly convex; the corona, a simple marginal wreath, notched ventrally; the foot small, ventrally placed, retractile, and with two small toes. The **mastax** (fig. 16 b) is globular, with a backward projecting part, like a stalk, containing the fulcrum. The trophi are of a forcipate pattern, and can be best understood from the above figure. The œsophagus is very long, thin, and expansible, exactly like that of *hyptopus* or *clavulatus*: the stomach is long, conical, sacculated, studded with globules, and with three ribbon-like cæcal projections on each side. The **gastric** glands are long cylindrical organs, bifurcate at their free ends. There is a good-sized **contractile vesicle**; and the lateral canals and vibratile tags are obvious. The **nervous ganglion** is small, lying between the eyes and the dorsal antenna; which latter is a mere setigerous pimple on the neck, with two threads passing to it from the nervous ganglion. Very powerful muscles pass from the head down the whole length of the body-cavity and are fastened at its base; thus completing a picture which might almost stand for that of *Notops clavulatus* itself.

Of course *lacustris* is not technically a *Notops*; its two frontal eyes appear to forbid its entrance into that genus, just as they seem to invite it into the genus *Diglena*. For all that, its true affinities are with *hyptopus* and *clavulatus*, for it is internally like the one, and externally like the other.

Length, $\frac{1}{70}$ inch. **Habitat.** Littleton, near London (Western).

COPEUS EHRENBERGII, *Ehrenberg* (Pl. XXXII. fig. 17).
Notommata eopeus . . . . . Ehrenberg (42).

SP. CH. *Front furnished with a pair of long thick cylindrical* **auricles**, *ciliated at the tips, projectile and retractile; lumbar regions with a stout* **seta** *on each side, projecting at right angles to the lateral surface;* **tail** *pointed, stiff; chin projecting moderately, ciliated;* **brain** *threefold.*

This fine Rotiferon is so like *C. labiatus*, when its auricles are withdrawn, that it might easily be mistaken for that animal. It differs from *labiatus* in the shape of the front; in the possession of large telegraph-like auricles; in the much smaller size of its ciliated lip; and in its foot having three joints instead of two. Moreover, Mr. Gosse, although he met with several specimens of *labiatus*, never found one with the gelatinous

c 2

covering which is generally present on *Ehrenbergii*. *C. pachyurus*, when its auricles are extended, has also a great resemblance to this *Copeus*; but the transparent bag-like membrane which hangs behind in folds, and seems to do duty for a tail, is very unlike the stiff tail of *Ehrenbergii*: the lumbar processes, too, of the former are mere stumps;[1] and its size only half that of the latter.

Length, $\frac{1}{16}$ inch. **Habitat.** Berlin (Ehr.).

ALBERTIA VERMICULUS, *Dujardin* (40), (Pl. XXXII. fig. 21).

SP. CII. **Body** *uniformly cylindrical, slightly tapering to a large, conical, undivided* **foot.**

The genus *Albertia* is due to Dujardin, who formed it to contain *A. vermiculus*, which he had found in the intestines of garden slugs and earthworms. The **corona** is reduced to a few cilia on a sort of hood, which is protruded from the front of the body. The **mastax** is forcipate. Four pedunculated bodies are attached to the alimentary canal: the two anterior, sac-like; the two posterior, kidney-shaped. Dujardin says that "they empty their contents into the intestine, and are refilled by it." The **ovary** is a long straight sac, with seldom more than four eggs at once. Fœtuses, more or less developed, are seen in the largest individuals. **Contractile vesicle** and four pairs of vibratile tags are plainly visible.

Length. From $\frac{1}{17}$ to $\frac{1}{50}$ inch. **Habitat.** In the intestines of slugs and earthworms.

TAPHROCAMPA SELENURA, *Gosse* (169), (Pl. XXXI. fig. 5).

[SP. CII. **Body** *thick towards the head, tapering towards the foot; marked with strong articulations like* T. annulosa; **brain** *opaque, with a distinct red eye on its inner side;* **caudal fork** *a wide crescent;* **trophi** *as in* Notommata aurita.

Since the note in vol. i., p. 17, I have made repeated examinations of this form, which, I am now convinced, has specific value. The crescent behind is glassy clear throughout, continuous with the body, not articulated; its form is that of the new moon when first visible. Cf. *Balatro calvus*, Claparède (15).

Length, $\frac{1}{100}$ inch. **Habitat.** Lacustrine. P.H.G.]

NOTOMMATA LIMAX, *Gosse* (171), (Pl. XXXI. fig. 6).

[SP. CII. **Body** *vermiform, integument soft;* **alimentary canal** *ample, thrown into apparent annulation by alternate constrictions and swellings;* **brain** *having a globose terminal bulb partly filled with opaque chalk masses, and partly with a large eye;* **foot-bulb** *contained within the body;* **toes** *long, slender, acute, decurved.*

The slug-like softness of the skin gives this species some resemblance to *Diglena permollis*; but it is less versatile in outline. The **brain** recalls *N. aurita*, the ample sac having a slender tube running through it occupied with opaque specks, and terminating in an ovate expansion. This is, in part, opaque with chalk deposits, and its rounded extremity is filled with a large crimson eye (fig. 6 c). There is a likeness to *N. cyrtopus* in the **toes**; but the general facies is very diverse. Swimming, it will suddenly augment its speed, by pushing out for an instant a pair of auricles. There is a distinct tuberculous **tail**. The whole animal is tinged with pale yellow.

Length, $\frac{1}{13}$ inch. **Habitat.** In *Utricularia*, from a lough near Carrick-on-Shannon, P.H.G.]

NOTOMMATA OVULUM, *Gosse* (169), (Pl. XXXI. fig. 7).

[SP. CII. *Very small;* **body** *globose, plump;* **dorsum** *gibbous;* **venter** *flat;* **brain** *clear;* **eye** *wanting;* **foot** *short;* **toes** *rather long, acute, decurved.*

---

[1] Mr. W. Chapman and Mr. G. Western have called my attention to the presence of a bunch of setæ on the lumbar processes of *pachyurus*.

This attractive little form has so much resemblance to *N. lacinulata*, that I have doubted whether it is not a variety of that species. There are, however, divergencies, important, if minute. It is very much rounder in all aspects; the toes are longer, uniformly diminishing to acute points, and decidedly decurved; no trace of eye could be discerned. It swims rapidly, but evenly; does not *spring*, and does not *twitch*; both which actions are so characteristic of *lacinulata*. Auricles (?) are occasionally pushed out. The front projects in a tubercle, halfway between which and the auricle on each side is a stiff seta. I have examined three specimens, two from Woolston, and one from Dundee.

Length, ₃⅟₁₀ inch. Habitat. Lacustrine. P.H.G.]

NOTOMMATA THEODORA, *Gosse* (171), (Pl. XXXI. fig. 8).

[SP. CII. Eye *small, quite frontal;* foot *slender, straight, protrusile to an immense length, or wholly retractile.*

A noble form, of great elegance, and of glassy clearness; colourless, save for a tinge of pale-orange in the tissues of the head (frequent in the kindred species), and the occasional hue of the contents of the stomach. The body has the massive aspect of the species named, but the position of the eye is notable, close to the frontal edge of an ample brain. The form and extreme versatility of the foot, too, are quite peculiar. Sometimes the body is truncate behind, and only the tips of the tiny toes are seen protruding from the hyaline cavity; when, with lightning suddenness, the foot, like a slender rod of glass, is shot out to a length equalling the whole trunk; and so carried, while the animal darts along with headlong swiftness. The only parallel to this that occurs to me, is the case of *Rotifer macrurus*. The toes are often turned suddenly, to the right or left, at a joint just above them, the long foot else preserving its perfect straightness. When smoothly swimming the front often appears as if auricles were on the point of developing; but I have not seen them extruded. In retraction the front often becomes pursed-in in the middle.

Length. When fully extended, about ₆⅟₁₀ inch. Habitat. Lacustrine. P.H.G.]

NOTOMMATA POTAMIS, *Gosse* (170), (Pl. XXXI. fig. 9).

[SP. CII. Body *sub-cylindric, gradually tapering to the foot;* brain *clear, obscurely three-lobed;* head *broad, with conspicuous oblique* auricles; trunk *strongly fluted;* foot *long;* toes *short, pointed.*

Having much in common with *N. Naias*, both in general form and in details, this presents characters which appear to mark it as specifically distinct. In more than a dozen examples which I have examined, alive and dead, from Woolston Pond and other waters, these distinctive features were seen. The auricles are large and strongly marked, extruded freely, and so remaining even in death, having the form, not of *hemispheres*, but of short truncated *columns*, thrust out *obliquely*, so as to make the whole head obconic. A great clear brain shows a tendency to triplicity; the middle sac bears a conspicuous red eye on its inner surface, above its swelling. The whole body is fluted strongly, about twelve deep incisions running longitudinally throughout, so that a transverse section would show so many rounded elevations. The stomach has a pair of minute ovate glands, is very large and saccate, with a distinct intestine. The last joint of the trunk forms a globose saccate sort of tail, over and behind the first joint of the foot, not unlike that of *Copeus pachyurus*. The branchial system displays thick convolute vessels, and a small contractile bladder. The whole animal, in life, is often tinged with delicate yellow, of deeper hue in the stomach. Several specimens, which seem to belong to this species, recently obtained (April 1887) from a pond near my residence, have the head of an orange hue, the front half of the mastax of a transparent

crimson, and the eye of a rich ruby-red ; the whole giving a most attractive appearance
to the animal, which is, moreover, very vivacious in manner.

Length, $_{v}^{1}$ inch. **Habitat.** Lacustrine. P.II.G.]

NOTOMMATA TORULOSA, *Dujardin* (40), (Pl. XXXII. fig. 20).

Lindia torulosa	Dujardin (40) ; Cohn (20).
Notommata roseola (?) . . .	Perty (124).
Notommata tardigrada (?) . .	Leydig (110).

SP. CII. **Body** *cylindrical, with several transverse constrictions, slightly tapering
at both ends, rounded in front ;* **auricles** *evertile and pedunculated ;* **toes** *very short ;*
brain *long, cylindrical, and ending in a rounded dark mass which is white by reflected
light.*

It is, I think, highly probable that a Rotiferon with these specific characters has been
described as a new species by three separate observers in succession, and has been named
differently by each of them. I shall follow Leydig's and Cohn's descriptions, which agree
in almost every particular ; only Leydig never saw the creature protrude its auricles.
The Rotiferon has a worm-like **body** ; a long, spheroidal **mastax** with forcipate trophi ;
a rather long **œsophagus** ; a long, straight stomach, ending in a short, clear, intestine ;
and a conspicuous, small **contractile vesicle.** Neither Leydig nor Cohn could see the
vibratile tags. The **nervous ganglion** is of the generic pattern, a long cylinder with a
rounded end stretching from the fore part of the head, over the mastax, to the top of the
stomach. This rounded end is, says Cohn, full of strongly refractive particles, which are
greyish-white by reflected light, and dark by transmitted light. In front of them lies, in
adults, a black **eye-spot** ; which in young individuals is red. Each **auricle,** according to
Cohn, is a roundish ciliated knob on a thin peduncle. The main differences between
Cohn and Leydig are due to the latter having had no opportunity of seeing the auricles,
and the former having overlooked some very fine short cilia which fringe the mouth,
a slit on the ventral surface of the head. A minor difference is that Leydig's animal was
$_{4}^{1}$ inch, while Cohn's was $_{v}^{1}$ inch, and Dujardin's $_{v}^{1}$ inch.

Cohn is of opinion that Perty's *N. roseola* is most probably the same animal ; and in
this I agree with him. It is true that his figure shows a stouter animal, with cylindrical
auricles ; but his description agrees closely with those of Cohn and Leydig, while all his
figures of Rotifera are rough and unsatisfactory. Both Cohn and Perty noticed that the
body had a faint pink tinge. This Rotiferon belongs evidently to the genus *Notommata,*
as defined by Mr. Gosse (*not* Ehrenberg), and I have of course added the specific name
torulosa devised by its discoverer Dujardin.

Length. Maximum observed, $_{4}^{1}$ inch ; minimum, $_{v}^{1}$ inch. **Habitat.** Among the
slime of the Maine (Leydig) ; pools and watercourses of the Aar towards Belp (Perty).

NOTOMMATA ONISCIFORMIS, *Perty* (124), (Pl. XXXII. fig. 19).

SP. CII. **Body** *very flatly arched, so as to resemble an Oniscus ;* **trophi** *stout ;*
uncus *with many teeth ;* **auricles** *round and small ;* **toes** *rather long.*

Perty says that the **cilia** lie between the auricles ; that the **eye** is red ; that the **uncus**
has many teeth ; and that he could see no organs, through the thick, striped, though
hyaline coat, but the eye, mastax, and alimentary canal. Mr. Gosse (vol. ii. p. 23) has
noticed the similarity of its cross-section to that of his *N. pilarius.*

Length, $_{1}^{1}_{4}$ inch. **Habitat.** Pools and watercourses of the Aar, towards Belp ;
among confervæ and charæ (Perty).

N. REINHARDTI = *F. Reinhardti,* Ehrenberg (12). SP. CII. **Body** *fusiform, truncated
in front ; a long cylindrical retractile* **foot,** *with short toes.* This is very closely allied

to Mr. Gosse's *Notommata Theodora*, if not identical with it. Each is of great trans-lucency; with a long, retractile, slender foot (equal in length to the trunk), minute toes, and a red frontal eye on an ample brain. They differ, however, in their habitats and habits. *Theodora* is a fresh-water species found among confervæ in a mill-stream, and "it darts along with headlong swiftness." *Reinhardti*, on the contrary, is only half the size of *Theodora*, is marine, parasitic on *Sertularia* and *Coryne*, and "its motion is not very lively." Length, $\frac{1}{90}$ inch.

N. CENTRURA, *Ehrenberg* (42). If Mr. Gosse's *Copeus labiatus* (vol. ii. p. 28) be deprived of its lumbar spines, and of its extraordinary lip, we should have precisely Ehrenberg's *N. centrura*; as, indeed, Leydig pointed out (110). Mr. Gosse thought it impossible that so good an observer as Ehrenberg could have overlooked the lip; and it is very difficult to suppose that he could have done so. But his figure has evidently been taken from an animal under pressure; and shows what look very much like two lumbar spines bent back, by the cover-glass, on to the body; and so pressed as to divide into the separate hairs of which they are composed. Under such circumstances the great lip might have been hidden by the head; and it is just possible that Ehrenberg did overlook it.

N. MELANOGLENA, N. MEGALADENA, N. SULCATA, *Schmarda* (195). See note 1, Sup*, p. 8.

PROALES WERNECKII, *Ehrenberg* (Pl. XXXII. fig. 18).

Notommata Werneckii. . . Ehrenberg (42); Balbiani (4, 5).

SP. CH. Body *fusiform, segmented by transverse folds, tapering continuously to front and rear; ventral ciliated face distinctly oblique; a slightly decurved* proboscis; toes *small, straight, pointed: parasitic in galls of* Vaucheria.

Although Ehrenberg established the fact that a Rotiferon lives in excrescences on the filaments of *Vaucheria*, he had no opportunity of studying the creature, as all his speci-mens died before they were hatched. Professor Balbiani, however, was more fortunate; and he has given (*loc. cit.*) an admirable account of the animal, and its habits, accom-panied by equally good drawings. It is from this account that the following remarks are taken.

The tubes of *Vaucheria* often bear two kinds of excrescences: the one, the organs of reproduction; the other, which are much larger, are generally club-shaped capsules, nearly at right-angles to the stem, and of the same green colour. These are the habita-tions of *N. Werneckii*, and Professor Balbiani is of opinion that they are the reproduc-tive organs of the plant, stimulated into excessive growth by the action on them of the saliva of the Rotiferon. (See Vol. ii., p. 134.)

The young animal is at first a free swimmer, and then, while still young, enters the plant by some opening in the reproductive capsule; either by the ordinary one in the male capsule, or by one at the summit of the altered cell. It remains in the cell for the rest of its life, feeding on the colourless plasma of the cell, and laying eggs.

The body is soft and fusiform, and divided by folds of the cuticle into segments capable of being retracted, one within the other. The head, on its dorsal surface, is prolonged into a projecting proboscis; and, on the ventral surface, is cut away obliquely, so that the profile tapers to the proboscis. The last segment of the body bears two small pointed toes. At the base of the proboscis a flap descends on either side, whose edge is ciliated; and these ciliated flaps surround the entrance to the buccal funnel, at the bottom of which lie the true mouth, and a ciliated organ, capable of protrusion, repre-senting the corona. This organ is excessively mobile, as is also the proboscis, but is made use of only in a very early stage of the animal's existence. The buccal funnel is long, the trophi virgate; and the salivary and gastric glands are unusually large. The communication, between these latter and the stomach, is gradually enlarged; and the gastric glands are ultimately drawn into it. The contractile vesicle is small, and the lateral canals are obvious ; but no vibratile tags have, as yet, been seen. The **nervous ganglion** is a pale, rounded, finely granulated mass, above the mastax ; and seated above its posterior border, in the neck, is the **eye** : a small crystalline, refractive lens, on a small mass of red pigment. Above the anterior border of the brain, is a small spherical pit in the dorsal surface, covered with fine vibratile cilia. The use of this organ is unknown. There is a simple **ovary**, which becomes much distended with eggs flattened by pressure against one another ; and after a time the ovisac appears to be ruptured, and the eggs fall into the general cavity of the body, which becomes much distorted. Professor Balbiani satisfied himself that the *same* female, while occupying, alone, the same capsule, laid first ordinary "summer" **eggs**, and then ephippial ones. Professor Balbiani has not seen the **male**, which at present is unknown.

   Length. About $\frac{1}{100}$ inch. **Habitat.** Galls of *Vaucheria*.

PROALES CORYNEGER, *Gosse* (171), (Pl. XXXI. fig. 10).

   [SP. CII. **Body** *nearly cylindrical, rounded in front and rear ; foot stout, apparently one-jointed ; toes two, furcate, rod-shaped, thick at base, tapering to an obtuse point, very slightly recurved, half as long as body-and-head.*

   This obscure form I cannot, on the evidence of a single specimen, identify with any species known to me ; though I own it presents little distinctive character. Its long, thick, club-shaped **toes** form its most obvious distinction ; these are usually carried *wide apart*. The figure suggests *Diaschiza* ; but I could not detect any dorsal fissure, and the soft skin seems destitute of a lorica. There is a minute red **eye** in the occiput. In swimming it is rapid, smoothly gliding ; darting to and fro, without any appreciable aim.

   Length, $\frac{1}{100}$ inch. **Habitat.** Kingskerswell, lacustrine. P.H.G.]

PROALES OTHODON, *Gosse* (170), (Pl. XXXI. fig. 11).

   [SP. CII. **Body** *nearly cylindrical, but arched in the line of the back, straight in that of the belly ; very plump throughout ;* **mastax** *forcibly protusile ;* **foot** *and* **toes** *minute.*

   This occurred in water from Woolston—a single example only. It is of plump hog-like form, without wrinkles, and almost without folds. It has no very marked characteristics, yet it does not seem referrible to any recognised species. There is a slight projection from the front in a lateral view, which, however, in a dorsal view appears to be a wide ridge seen endwise. The face is obliquely prone, from the midst of which the **jaws** are occasionally protruded, with force, in the manner of a fierce *Diglena* : the details of these jaws I was not able to trace. A sac-like **brain** is conspicuous, but I could discern no **eye**. The **stomach** and distinct intestine are ample ; the former carries a pair of gastric **glands**, which are large, high, and pointed.

   Length, $\frac{1}{100}$ inch. **Habitat.** Woolston, lacustrine. P.H.G.]

PROALES PREHENSOR, *Gosse* (170), (Pl. XXXI. fig. 12).

   [SP. CII. **Body** *bottle- or oil-flask-shaped, but with the belly nearly flat ; fore parts long, very protusile ;* **eye** *small ;* **face** *prone ; a short tuberculous tail ;* **foot** *short ;* **toes** *blade-shaped, straight, acute, usually appressed.*

   I have doubts where I should place this species. Technically, it seems a *Notommata* or *Proales*, with the form of a *Distyla*, yet having much in common with *Distemma*. The **toes**, in particular—blades, widest in the middle, with slender produced tips, and generally carried close together as one (though sometimes widely spread)—remind us forcibly of *Distyla* or *Cathypna*. The **trophi**, too, suggest the same alliance : viewed ventrally, the length and form of the mallei, and the triradiate incus, for instance :— yet I believe I have seen a great blade-like prolongation of the incus arching far into the occiput ; and, at times, what seemed a short forcipate form of the unci, as in *Diglena* and *Distemma*. There appears a sort of **proboscis**, but close appressed, not at all movable. I have never seen the **jaws** protruded, though they are every moment brought to the bottom of the ciliate face, snapping up atoms of food.

It is not much given to locomotion, but can swim, rather slowly : usually, it rolls hither and thither, or adheres by the toes. It picks industriously among the vegetable floccose for morsels of food : it is vivacious and energetic, and altogether attractive ; constantly reminding me of the marine *Distemma raptor*. I have observed, in all, about a score of examples, all isolated.

Length, $\frac{1}{13}$ inch. **Habitat.** Woolston, lacustrine. P.H.G.]

FURCULARIA LACTISTES, *Gosse* (171), (Pl. XXXI. fig. 13).

[SP. CII. **Back** *much arched, soft and plump, smooth, round;* **foot** *stout;* **toes** *long, slender, acute, decurved; foot and toes together equal in length to the trunk; a short pointed* **tail.**

It possesses much elegance of form, and a most restless activity, every instant retrojecting the long foot and toes, with the action of a kicking horse, very forcibly and pertinaciously. It has one very curious habit : it constantly insinuates itself between two stalks of conferva, where it immediately begins to make itself a cell (only just large enough to hold it) by incessantly turning head over heels. As soon as it has got its place, it bends the front down to the belly, and begins to roll round and round, without a moment's cessation for hours. If forced out, it at once begins the same process somewhere else. The habit, which is not that of an individual, but is characteristic of the species, may be compared with the tube-making propensity of *F. forficula* (vol. ii. p. 41). In other respects it has the manners of its genus ; as in its sudden and rapid motions, its volutions, and its swift shooting way of swimming. The **incus-fulcrum** appeared to be a massive pillar, with long, slender, divergent, arching rami : the mallei, evanescent.

I met with several examples of this interesting species, inhabiting floating tufts of a floccose conferva, that waved in a rapid rivulet in the village of Kingskerswell. And, a few weeks later, two more occurred in water from Carrick-on-Shannon. These had the same form, and identically the same habits, as the Devonshire specimens. More recently, I have detected the same species in other waters.

Length, $\frac{1}{15}$ inch. **Habitat.** Lacustrine. P.H.G.]

FURCULARIA MOLARIS, *Gosse* (171), (Pl. XXXI. fig. 14).

[SP. CII. **Body** *ovate, with a thick truncate head, and suddenly diminishing to a long foot, terminated by two blade-shaped, straight, acute,* **toes** *; back elevated; belly straight.*

A single round **eye**, well-defined, of ruby brilliance, near the frontal part of a clear saccate brain, marks this rather insignificant species. The **trophi** are nearly as in *F. lactistes* just described ; but the mallei are more developed. An ample **alimentary canal**, undivided, nearly fills the trunk ; and a clear **ovary** crosses it obliquely, having in general embryonic vesicles more or less conspicuous. The long **foot** and toes are carried straight behind, and both extended are about as long as the trunk. It is, as usual, restless, moderately swift, with a smooth gliding course. It is an elegant and attractive little species, which, for lack of any marked characteristics, I name from the locality in which I found it—the Kingskerswell mill-stream. Here, on different occasions, I have met with several examples.

Length, $\frac{1}{15}$ inch. **Habitat.** Lacustrine. P.H.G.]

FURCULARIA STREFA, *Gosse* (171), (Pl. XXXI. fig. 15).

[SP. CII. **Body** *ovato-cylindric, with a thick truncate head, and sub-prone face; behind ending in a short, decurved, acute* **tail** *;* **foot** *short and thick, apparently one-jointed;* **toes** *moderate, acute, scarcely decurved.*

Having much in common with *F. molaris*, this is quite diverse in facies and habit. The head is of nearly the same thickness as the trunk; the little overarching tail (seemingly a stiff point), and the short but massive foot, are differences that strike one at first sight. The **eye** is distinct, quite prominently frontal; immediately beneath it the **face** recedes, and becomes a sub-prone ciliate surface, applied to the feeding-ground. It it much larger than *F. molaris*. The single specimen seen had a great **contractile vesicle**, and a small undeveloped **ovary**. The **stomach** seemed undivided. The fore-parts were tinged of a delicate yellow hue. It was not much addicted to swimming, but crept vivaciously about the vegetation, grubbing and browsing.

Length, $\frac{1}{13}$ inch. **Habitat.** A pond in Watcombe Park, Torquay. P.II.G.]

FURCULARIA SPHÆRICA, *Gosse* (171), (Pl. XXXI. fig. 16).

[SP. CII. **Body** *glebose dorsally, nearly flat ventrally;* **foot** *short, thick;* **toes** *small, straight, acute; the dorsum projecting over them with a slight rim or margin, which, laterally seen, looks like a* **tail.**

In lateral aspect this pleasing little form may easily be mistaken for a deep *Colurus,* till the **trophi** reveal its true Furcularian character, confirmed by a minute ruby **eye** at the extreme front; as also by its motions. The **head** seems not retractile. I first formed acquaintance with it, in half-a-dozen examples on different occasions, from tide-pools in the Firth of Tay. Then a specimen, recently dead, occurred in fresh-water among *Myriophyllum,* thickly studded with *Melicerta ringens* and *Floscularia cornuta.* And presently, to confirm the amphibious habitat, I found one alive in *Utricularia* from a lough in the centre of Ireland. These fresh-water specimens I could in nowise distinguish from the marine.

Length, $\frac{1}{215}$ inch. **Habitat.** Marine and lacustrine. P.II.G.]

FURCULARIA EVA, *Gosse* (171), (Pl. XXXI. fig. 17).

[SP. CH. **Body** *stout, fusiform, strongly elevated on the shoulder;* **foot** *short, indistinct;* **toes** *more than half as long as body-and-head, thick for half this length, then abruptly attenuated for the remainder.*

The great length and peculiar form of the toes, which are often thrown back, and carried over the back, give a facies to this rather fine species, which at once strikes an observer. Sometimes these organs are extended in opposite directions in a horizontal line, imparting to the animal the figure of the letter T reversed. The **mastax** is ample; the incus a thick rod, bent in the middle backwards, and ending occipitally in a pair of long and broad scythe-shaped processes; the mallei indistinct. A slender **brain** descends behind; but no **eye** is visible, unless two very pale globules, close side by side, in the very front, are such.

A single specimen only has occurred, whose activity mainly consisted in the vigorous throwing into different positions of the characteristic toes.

Length, $\frac{1}{113}$ inch. **Habitat.** Mill stream, Kingskerswell. P.II.G.]

FURCULARIA LOPHYRA, *Gosse* (169), (Pl. XXXI. fig. 19).

[SP. CII. **Body** *fusiform;* **head** *separated by a constriction; back sharply ridged;* **toes** *broad at base, tapering at mid-length to long-drawn fine points.*

Somewhat near to *F. gracilis,* but the above characters, which are constant in a great number of examples, sufficiently distinguish it. The **body,** sub-cylindric at first, swells more or less behind the middle, where the dorsum rises to a sharp edge, *not a carina.* The **head** is large, always distinct, with a brilliant **eye** at the very front, and a prone ciliate **face.** The **trophi** are those of *gracilis,* very large, often extruded. A thick short **foot** bears two great **toes** (often widely expanded) one-fourth of the whole length;

each is a glassy rod, of thick base, which tapers somewhat abruptly near the middle to a long point of great tenuity.

Length, $\frac{1}{200}$ to $\frac{1}{300}$ inch. **Habitat.** Lacustrine. P.H.G.]

FURCULARIA MELANDOCUS, *Gosse* (169), (Pl. XXXI. fig. 18).

[SP. CH. **Body** *swollen, obtusely narrowed in front, tapering behind ;* **brain** *saccate, opaque at the extremity ;* **foot** *large ;* **toes** *conical, each terminating in a soft, slender point, much produced.*

Of excessively versatile outline, rapidly lengthening and shortening every instant. The **front** is apparently hard, with a sharp edge, below which is a broad, sub-prone, ciliate face. An ample **brain-sac**—its terminal portion filled with chalky deposit, usually intensely black by transmitted light, but in some examples much diluted—looks like a bottle of ink swaying to and fro in the animal's contortions.

The prolonged finger-like tips of the **toes** have a strong adhesive power, dependent on a pair of great mucus-glands. A minute frontal **eye** is not *quite* certain.

Length, $\frac{1}{130}$ inch. **Habitat.** Woolston pond ; several examples. P.H.G.]

EOSPHORA NAIAS, *Ehrenberg* (42), (Pl. XXXIII. fig. 9).

SP. CH. **Body** *hyaline, conical, not auricled ;* **toes** *much shorter than the foot.*

Ehrenberg says that the internal structure resembles that of *Hydatina,* except that the **mallei** are one-toothed, and that he failed to find either an **antenna** or **vibratile tags.** The **brain** is large, lies higher up than the mastax, and carries a transversely-oval red **eye.** There are also two paler red spots on prominences on the frontal edge of the head : these Ehrenberg considers to be eyes, but Leydig (110) maintains that they are nothing but spots of a deeper orange hue than the rest of the edge of the corona ; and that *naias* is a true *Notommata,* with only one eye, in the neck. Herr Eckstein (41), however, agrees with Ehrenberg as to the nature of the spots. I have given Leydig's figure, which is much more characteristic than Ehrenberg's, and shows the forcipate trophi, and the frontal prominences, on the inner side of which the red spots are situated.

Length, $1\frac{1}{10}$ to $\frac{1}{16}$ inch. **Habitat.** Berlin (Ehr.).

EOSPHORA DIGITATA, *Ehrenberg* (12), (Pl. XXXIII. fig. 10).

SP. CH. **Body** *hyaline, conical, not auricled ;* **toes** *one-third of length of foot.* Very similar to *naias,* but with longer toes.

Length, $\frac{1}{16}$ inch. **Habitat.** Berlin ; among confervæ (Ehr.).

EOSPHORA ELONGATA, *Ehrenberg* (42), (Pl. XXXIII. fig. 8).

SP. CH. **Body** *elongated, almost fusiform, slender, truncate in front ;* **toes** *short.*

Ehrenberg gives no more information about this animal than what may be derived from his SP. CH., and his drawings. He had found it in 1831, and had drawn it ; but had not met with it again. Herr Eckstein, however, (41) has carefully described and figured this Rotiferon ; and from his description the following account is derived. The **trunk** is of an ovoid shape, with a distinctly separate head. The **corona** consists of two wreaths of rather long cilia, among which are two spots with still larger setæ. The three-lobed **mastax** lies behind and below the brain, the trophi are stout, and the œsophagus is long and curved. The spherical **stomach** bears not only the usual gastric **glands** but also a third very large gland, which crosses its middle as a transverse, broad ring, divided by deep incisions into anastomosing parts.[1] The two **foot-glands** have each a long tube leading to the end of the toes. The **nervous ganglion,** or brain, is three-

[1] This is, I think, an error. See the explanation of a similar mistake in the description of *Triophthalmus dorsualis,* Sup', p. 32.

lobed and bears a great red **eye** ; two smaller red spots are borne on prominences in the front of the head ; and on each side of the body, about the middle, is a rocket-shaped **antenna**, like those in *Hydatina senta*. A **contractile vesicle**, lateral canals, vibratile tags, and **ovary** are also present.

Herr Eckstein says that this creature preys on other Rotifera ; and he vividly describes how he has seen a *Monostyla* drawn by the vortex of *elongata*'s cilia into its buccal funnel, and there slit up by the teeth and devoured.

Length, $\frac{1}{17}$ inch. **Habitat.** Berlin (Ehr.).

E. CARIBÆA, *Schmarda* (135). See note 1, Sup^t, p. 8.

DIGLENA CONURA, Ehrenberg (42), (Pl. XXXIII. fig. 11).

SP. CII. **Body** *ovately oblong, front transversely truncate, the hinder part of the body gradually diminishing to a conical foot.*

This *Diglena* somewhat resembles *catellina*, but lacks its plump, dorsal rotundity. The **foot**, too, is differently placed ; being in a line with the long axis of the body, instead of being placed ventrally beneath it. The only difference (according to Ehrenberg) in the internal structure is that the **gastric glands** are almost hemispherical, while those of *catellina* are spherical.

Length, $\frac{1}{117}$ inch. **Habitat.** Berlin (Ehr.).

DIGLENA CAPITATA, Ehrenberg (42), (Pl. XXXIII. fig. 12).

SP. CII. **Body** *oblong, conical, with an obliquely truncate and dilated front, gradually diminishing behind to two toes, and apparently baseless,* **toes.**

Ehrenberg says but little of this species, which is mainly distinguished by its broad head, conical body, and long **toes.** These latter seem to spring at once, without the interposition of a single joint, from the base of the body itself. The **mastax** is long ; the **mallei** one-toothed ; the **gastric glands** spherical.

Length, $\frac{1}{316}$ inch. **Habitat.** Near Berlin (Ehr.).

DIGLENA AQUILA, Gosse (171), (Pl. XXXI. fig. 20).

[**SP. CII.** **Body** *fusiform ;* **head** *furnished with a beak ;* **foot** *short, thick ;* **toes** *nearly as long as trunk, thick to half-length, then diminishing to stiff, straight rods with obtuse points.*

The long, straight, blunt **toes** are very characteristic. The **proboscis** is a broad shield, somewhat as in *Stephanops*, permanent, surrounded by a ring of very long vibratile cilia. It forms, indeed, a hooked beak, shaped like that of an eagle, the edges of which converging to a point (fig. 20 c) are distinctly visible from above, through its hyaline substance.

In manners it is headstrong, abrupt, vigorous ; most restless, never pursuing one course more than an instant, but suddenly stopping, and turning round on itself, augmenting its speed greatly for a moment, rushing, or rather *shooting*, forward for three or four times its length, then again and again, but never springing sidewise. I first received it from the middle of Ireland, by the kindness of Mr. Hood junr.; then in a pond near my own residence ; and on several occasions since. It bears a very close resemblance to a species discovered by Mr. E. C. Bousfield, of which he courteously sent me a drawing, under the name of *Notommata rapax*. This has two conspicuous styles (antennæ ?) projecting straight from the head, which I do not see in *D. aquila*. If, however, the two are identical, his specific name has the priority. None of my earlier examples showed any trace of an **eye-spot** ; but I have met with a specimen, in another missive from Mr. Hood junr., in which was conspicuous a very large black occipital eye, if, indeed, it was not an opaque chalk-mass of the brain.

Length, $\frac{1}{45}$ inch. **Habitat.** Babbacombe ; Ireland. P.H.G.]

DIGLENA ROSA, *Gosse* (171), (Pl. XXXI. fig. 21).

[SP. CH. **Body** *lengthened, fusiform, annulose, larva-like ;* **proboscis** *frontal, beak-shaped, within which are two colourless* **eyes** ; **foot** *minute ;* **toes** *small, straight, acute.*

The strong division of the body into annular false joints recalls *Taphrocampa.* The head, too, resembles that of an insect-larva. The frontal **beak** is broadly triangular, like that of *D. aquila* just described, and its sharp point, hooked downward, can be seen from above, through its transparent substance. Two well-defined, perfectly colourless bodies, side by side, are also seen through the base of the beak, apparently **eyes** without pigment. A ring of close-set cilia surrounds the front, behind the base of the beak. The **face** is truncate, studded with warty eminences. The body terminates in a distinct, bulbous tail.

Several examples occurred in conferva-tufts waving in the swift mill-stream in Kingskerswell. All were of a clear horn-yellow hue, with the long alimentary canal full of opaque food-matter. They were restless and swift ; the jaws often protruded from the face, *more generis.* The beak was much more acute and better shaped in some, than in others.

Length, $\frac{1}{130}$ to $\frac{1}{115}$ inch. **Habitat.** Lacustrine. P.H.G.]

DIGLENA SUILLA, *Gosse* (170), (Pl. XXXI. fig. 24).

[SP. CH. **Body** *cylindric, or fusiform, massive, often gibbous in the middle ;* **face** *broad, sub-prone, with small, tubercular frontal* **proboscis** ; **eye** *large, cervical ;* **foot** *thick, short ;* **toes** *minute, decurved.*

This thick-bodied, plump, snouted, swine-like creature occurred in a number of examples, among conferva much crowded with groups of diatoms, in sea-water from Invergowrie. The **body** rises into successive swellings, divided by sharp constrictions like that of a full-fed caterpillar, diminishing abruptly to an oblique thick head, with a distinct round pimple in front, in which is a very minute refractive corpuscle, like a glass bead. This, however, is probably not an eye, the true **eye** being large and conspicuous, near the tip of an ample brain. The **front** is truncate, but appears semi-prone, from the inclination of the head ; it is ciliated on its whole surface, the cilia *surrounding* the globose proboscis, not *covering* it.

The **jaws** are of the same form as in other *Diglenæ,* as *permollis* ; viewed laterally, they are produced into a long point, which is often deliberately projected and retracted. Young specimens lack the plumpness of adults, especially in the hinder parts. The **stomach** is of great size, usually gorged with green granular food. The animal, in habit, is very sluggish.

Length, $\frac{1}{200}$ inch. **Habitat.** Invergowrie ; marine. P.H.G.]

DIGLENA (?) PACHIDA, *Gosse* (170), (Pl. XXXI. fig. 23).

[SP. CH. **Body** *thick, sub-cylindric, very variable in outline ;* **skin** *leathery, thrown into strong folds ;* **eye** *wanting ;* **toes** *two, furcate, long, slender, acute, decurved.*

Several examples of this curious thickset form, more remarkable than attractive, occurred to me last summer, in sea-water from various rock-pools in Torbay. It is uncouth, heavy, and sluggish, apparently illoricate, but inclosed in an integument which seems of leathery stiffness, making stout, transverse folds, whence the fore and hind parts project at intervals. The **head,** at extreme protrusion, shows a thread-like frontal proboscis, an ample **brain,** but no eye, and **trophi** which appear slight and very simple, but need further examination. The **toes,** long and slender, have that backward direction which is seen in many *Diglenæ,* yet have a forward curve. The internal organs are nearly lost in an indistinguishable granulation.

Its generic affinities are very doubtful. It is not improbable that a more matured acquaintance may elevate this strange form to the rank of a genus. In any case it is a notable addition to our marine Rotifera.

Length, $\frac{3}{17}$ **inch. Habitat.** Rock-pools, Torbay; marine. P.H.G.]

DIGLENA (?) SILPHA, *Gosse* (169), (Pl. XXXI. fig. 22).

[**SP. CII. Body** *sub-cylindric, stouter at the head, abruptly lessened behind ;* **brain** *saccate, long, opaque at the end ;* **toes** *minute, conical.*

The whole animal is very soft and plump, not wrinkled, even in retraction. A well-marked, soft, decurved **proboscis** is on the front : no **eye** is visible. The sudden attenuation of the body to a slender cylinder, one-fourth of the whole length, is remarkable : this terminates in two or three soft lobes, below which are two very minute **toes**, with no appreciable foot intervening ; for the rectum can be traced to a cloaca just above the toes. Fuller examination is needed : I have seen but a single example, and the **trophi** were not satisfactorily defined. Cf. *Notommata forcipata,* lateral aspect.

Length, $\frac{1}{100}$ **inch. Habitat.** Ireland ; lacustrine. P.H.G.]

DIGLENA (?) UNCINATA, *Milne* (186), (Pl. XXXIII. fig. 13).

SP. CII. **Body** *sub-cylindric, gibbous dorsally behind ; ciliated* **face** *oblique, and overhung by a hood ;* **foot** *very short, with two very long, decurved and divergent, blade-like* **toes** *;* **eyes** *absent.*

The truncated **face** is covered with strong cilia ; two, or two pencils, of which are more than double the length of the rest, which are themselves longer than usual. The **nervous ganglion** is large, and below it lies an ovoid **mastax**, with a very formidable pair of protrusile three-toothed jaws. There is a very distensible " clear-walled " **œsophagus**, often wrinkled up, but sometimes so distended with food as to occupy half the body below the mastax, and so push down the true **stomach**.[1] This latter has two large, flat, wedge-shaped **glands**, each containing a peculiar vesicular hollow surrounded by two or three dozen granules. The **ovary** is large, extending up to the **mastax**, and developing eggs of a great size. The **vascular system** is normal ; at least two vibratile tags are readily seen behind the mastax. Two **foot-glands** lie just at the insertion of the toes ; and a short, fine seta springs from the " posterodorsal " surface of the foot, but is exceedingly difficult to detect. " This little creature has a curious way, when moving along, of suddenly, and with exceeding quickness, switching itself back on its toe-points, head over and back again, the motion being somewhat comparable, in its quickness and unexpectedness, to the springing of the Infusorian *Halteria grandinella.*"

The above characteristics and description have been taken from Mr. Milne's memoir (*loc. cit.*). The author shows clearly the close relation between this species and the next, which was described by him under the title of *Pleurotrocha mustela.* Like Mr. Milne, I hesitate where to place these two eyeless Diglenoid Rotifera ; but on the whole I agree with Mr. Gosse, that their trophi and their energetic habits ought to weigh more than the presence or absence of eye specks ; and that they should be placed in the genus *Diglena.*

Length, $\frac{1}{100}$ **inch.**

DIGLENA MUSTELA, *Milne* (Pl. XXXIII. fig. 14).

Pleurotrocha mustela . . . . . Milne (188).

SP. CII. *Like the preceding, but with very short* **toes**.

There are one or two other points in which the two species differ. The **gastric glands**, in *mustela*, are pyriform, and attached to the (true) stomach by long stalks.

---

[1] See *Triophthalmus dorsalis*, p. 32.

There are no ciliated tufts, in the **corona**, longer than the rest ; there is a blunt dorsal **antenna** protected by the hood ; and the **vibratile tags** are sufficiently inconspicuous to have escaped observation. The creature is fierce and active : if it strikes an object with its jaws, it hangs on and sucks like a weasel, even when whirled round by its prey. Infusoria are often attacked by it, and will tear themselves out of its grasp, leaving pieces of their bodies in its jaws. Once Mr. Milne saw it make so desperate a snatch at its prey, that it locked its rami together into a straight line ; and, unable to unlock them, died of its fatal greediness. It often swallowed a *Glaucoma* ; and on one occasion devoured no fewer than six (or half its own bulk) in less than an hour. All of these were digested in the large œsophagus (see *D. uncinata*), and in an hour and a half there was nothing left but a pulpy mass, which had not yet reached the true stomach.

Mr. Milne has also seen and described the **male**. It is a much smaller animal than the female, more elongated, and with a more developed hood. Its structure is normal.[1]

Length, (of female) $\frac{1}{100}$ to $\frac{1}{140}$ inch ; (of male) $\frac{1}{180}$ inch.

D. ANDESINA, D. DIADEMA, D. LONGIPES, D. MACRODONTA, *Schmarda* (185) ; see note 1, Sup^t, p. 8.

D. GRANULARIS, *Weisse* (41)=*D. catellina*.

DISTEMMA FORFICULA, *Ehrenberg* (12), (Pl. XXXIII. fig. 19).

SP. CH. **Body** *cylindrically conical;* **toes** *stout, re-curved, toothed at the base ;* **eyes** *red.*

Ehrenberg says but little of this Rotiferon. He thinks it closely related to *Furcularia forficula* ; and notices that the two red **eyes** are situated at the end of a long cylindrical brain.

Length, $\frac{1}{120}$ inch. **Habitat.** Near Berlin (Ehr.).

DISTEMMA PLATYCEPS, *Gosse* (171), (Pl. XXXI. fig. 25).

[SP. CH. **Body** *subfusiform ;* **belly** *flat ;* **head** *broadly truncate ;* **eyes** *two colourless globules, remote, occipital ;* **foot** *rounded ;* **toes** *taper, acute, slightly decurved.*

Though not unlike certain conditions of *Diglena suilla* and *permollis*, this is distinguished by its two large colourless **eyes** ; and by the fact that while the **trophi** are of the usual calliper form, the mallei are (or *seem*) attached to the bases rather than to the ends of the circular rami ; while the fulcrum is nearly as long as the mallei. An inconspicuous hooked **proboscis** is present, which appears retractile. The broad **face** is of hyaline delicacy, free from corrugations and marks, as if clear gelatinous flesh, and this well defined from surrounding tissues, in all aspects.

Young specimens are very restless and mobile, but an adult was of slow movement. Five or six examples occurred to me in water from a tide-pool near Carnoustie, in Forfarshire. In the one the jaws were about half extruded from the face, and (as if by paralysis) could not be retracted, or even moved : an accident, the occurrence of which I have observed on repeated occasions, in predatory Rotifera. The species was numerous also in a ditch near Goodrington, South Devon.

Length, $\frac{1}{144}$ inch. **Habitat.** Marine and lacustrine. P.H.G.]

D. SETIGERUM, *Ehrenberg* (42), (Pl. XXXIII. fig. 18). SP. CH. "**Body** *ovato-oblong ;* **toes** *decurved, seta-like ;* **eyes** *red.*" Mr. Gosse points out (vol. ii. p. 54) that this Rotiferon belongs to the *Rattulidæ* ; and possibly (vol. ii. p. 70), in spite of the two cervical eyes assigned to it by Ehrenberg, to his new genus *Cœlopus*. Ehrenberg gives no account of its internal structure, and says hardly anything about it, except that one

---

[1] The whole of the above account of these two species is derived from Mr. Milne's able and exhaustive paper (*loc. cit.*).

toe lay inside the other, so that the two appeared to be one. Further investigation will be necessary to determine this Rotiferon's true position.

Length, $_2\frac{1}{6}$ inch. **Habitat.** Near Berlin (Ehr.).

D. (?) MARINUM, *Ehrenberg* (42), (Pl. XXXIII. fig. 16). SP. CII. "**Body** *ovato-conic ;* **foot** *long ;* **toes** *stout, equal in length to the foot ;* **eyes** *close together, red.*" Ehrenberg marks this as a doubtful species ; and indeed it resembles the rest of the genus in only one point, viz. in having two cervical **eyes.** These are closely pressed together, so as to look somewhat like those of a *Brachionus.* The trophi, too, have five teeth in each malleus, and are very unlike those of *D. raptor* (Pl. XIX. fig. 1 *b*). Ehrenberg's drawing seems also to show the presence of a transparent lorica, with a round opening for the foot. It is obvious that this Rotiferon must be more carefully observed, in order that its proper position may be assigned to it.

Length, $_1\frac{1}{4}$ inch. **Habitat.** Baltic Sea (Ehrenberg and Eichwald [1]).

D. (?) FORCIPATUM, *Ehrenberg* (42), (Pl. XXXIII. fig. 17). SP. CH. "**Body** *ovato-oblong ;* **foot** *short ;* **toes** *thick ;* **eyes** *colourless.*" A doubtful species, scarcely described at all, and feebly drawn. Ehrenberg merely says of it that it is vehement in its motions, and predaceous.

Length, about $_2\frac{1}{50}$ inch. **Habitat.** Near Berlin (Ehr.).

Genus TRIOPHTHALMUS, *Ehrenberg.*

GEN. CII. "*One of the* NOTOMMATADÆ, *with the three cervical* **eyes** *in a transverse row, and a forked* **foot.**"

TRIOPHTHALMUS DORSUALIS, *Ehrenberg* (42), (Pl. XXXIII. fig. 20).

Ehrenberg merely says of this fine Rotiferon (which is the only species of the genus) that its **body** is hyaline, swollen, and with a suddenly diminished foot, half as long as the body ; that it resembles *Notommata ansata* in form, and *Asplanchna myrmeleo* in size ; and that he regrets his having observed and drawn it under too low a power.

Mr. Gosse met with it once, and says, in a manuscript note, that "the **front** is pale orange, the **brain** saccate, and the **eyes** in a row near (not *at*) the end of the brain. Over the foot hangs a bulbous joint, which looks, laterally, like a **tail.** The creature resembles a stout-built *Notommata aurita* or *naias.*"

M. Eckstein (41) gives a large figure of *dorsualis*, in which the internal structure is distinctly displayed ; and describes an additional **gastric gland** lying in a cluster of folds, close round the stomach, and containing many large clear vesicles. I think that M. Eckstein has, here, mistaken the thick-celled walls of the true stomach for a gastric gland ; and has considered a distended portion of the œsophagus to be part of the true stomach. I have often seen *Synchæta tremula*, *Notops hyptopus*, and *Notops clavulatus* with a portion (and even the whole) of the long œsophagus, so fully distended with food, that it was continuous with the stomach ; and so had the precise appearance of M. Eckstein's drawing. For, owing to the delicate thinness of the œsophageal walls, and the thickness of those of the stomach, when both become stuffed with a continuous mass of food, the stomach cells seem to be in a thick belt round that mass, and show off their oil globules to advantage on the dark ground.

M. Eckstein adds, that of the three cervical **pigment spots**, the centre one only is completely rounded, and that those on either side of it seem incomplete towards the inner edge. Mr. Gosse's drawing, too, confirms this observation. But M. Eckstein has also seen two red spots on the top of two low frontal prominences. These Mr. Gosse failed

---

[1] Unfortunately Eichwald's account of this creature (43) adds nothing whatever to that of Ehrenberg.

to find, as both he and I have failed to find many similar spots, seen by Mr. Eckstein, on the heads of various Rotifera.

Length, $\frac{1}{55}$ to $\frac{1}{45}$ inch (Ehrenberg); $\frac{1}{44}$ inch (P.II.G.); $\frac{1}{100}$ inch (Eckstein). **Habitat.** Watcombe (P.II.G.).

Family SEISONIDÆ, *Plate* (192).

Elongate vermiform animals, $\frac{1}{16}$ to $\frac{1}{8}$ inch in length, of similar form in both sexes ; the males somewhat smaller, and less abundant, than the females. The **body** is divided into four apparent segments, viz. the head, neck, middle body (trunk), and foot ; these, with the exception of the last two, are sharply separated from each other. The neck can be retracted in its whole length into the trunk, along its ventral surface. The corona is rudimentary or wanting. The buccal funnel and œsophagus meet at the anterior end of the mastax, which is thus a sacciform ventral appendage of the œsophagus. In the head, two dorsal and two ventral, long-stalked, pyriform **glands** empty their secretion before, or into, the mastax. Similar cells exist in the hind head and neck. **Stomach** elongated, formed of non-ciliated polygonal cells, and with two gastric **glands** in front. **Sexual organs** paired, with a common dorsal evacuator ; that of the male opening at the junction of neck and trunk ; that of the female, at the posterior extremity of the trunk. **Ovaries** consisting of numerous distinctly separated ova. The **male sexual** apparatus complicated ; having various parts, which may be regarded as seminal vesicle, *vas deferens*, and *ductus ejaculatorius*. Two lateral canals, furnished with vibratile tags, traverse head, neck, and trunk ; and discharge themselves externally, with the sexual organs. There is a dorsal **nervous ganglion** in the head, bearing a dorsal antenna : there are no lateral antennæ. The longitudinal **muscles** are strong, the transverse feeble ; none are striated. The **tail** has a number of long-stalked, pyriform, viscous glands, opening at the hind extremity of the foot. At the same point, towards the ventral surface, there is a vesicle opening by a short, projecting canal, the signification of which is doubtful.

The animals are ectoparasites on *Nebaliæ* of the Mediterranean and North Sea ; especially on their branchial laminæ. Ephippial eggs do not occur.

Genus SEISON, *Grube* (172).

With an **intestine** discharging itself with the excretory organ ; so that the anal aperture is situated differently in the two sexes. Corona two tufts of cilia placed on the anterior extremity. In the posterior half of the head 5–6 flask-shaped cells ; the efferent duct of which passes into the fore part of the neck. **Sexual organs** of the female placed ventrally to the stomach. The lateral canals do not fork in the trunk. The *ductus ejaculatorius* of the male possesses well-developed muscles in its walls, and performs undulatory movements. On the right side it forms a lobiform diverticulum ; and opposite to this, on the left side, a multipartite glandular body. No spermatophores. The foot terminates posteriorly in an adhesive disc. The whole ventral surface of the trunk is covered with a great number of transverse muscular fibres, and thereby acquires a striated appearance. In the Adriatic near Trieste.

Seison Grubei, *Claus* (17), (Pl. XXX. fig. 4).

SP. CII. **Trunk** *not annulated ;* **neck** *formed of three segments.* See vol. ii. p. 134.

Seison annulatus, *Claus* (18).

SP. CII. **Trunk** *divided into a large portion, and, following this, four short joints ;* the **neck** *shows more than three rings.*

D

Genus PARASEISON, *Plate* (192).

Both sexes without **intestine**. **Corona** as in *Seison*, or reduced to a few tactile setæ, or entirely wanting. In the hind head only two flask-shaped **glands**, which open into the œsophagus, in the commencement of the neck. **Sexual organs** in male and female placed laterally or dorsally to the stomach ; only exceptionally displaced below it. Each lateral canal with five vibratile tags, and giving off a thin-walled, cœcally terminating, lateral branch, in the anterior part of the trunk. The *ductus ejaculatorius* of the **male** with smooth walls, with no movements or lateral organs, with numerous flask-shaped spermatophores. The **foot** does not terminate with an adhesive disc, but the hind extremity of the foot has the form of a hemisphere beset with a row of small denticles, between which the viscous glands discharge themselves. In the Bay of Naples.

PARASEISON ASPLANCHNUS, *Plate* (192), (Pl. XXXIII. fig. 22).

SP. CII. *Average size of the adult* **female** ₂½₃ *inch. Without true* **corona**, *but with four tufts of tactile setæ, standing round the buccal aperture.*

PARASEISON NUDUS, *Plate* (192).

SP. CH. *Size* ₇⅟₅ *inch.* **Head** *without any trace whatever of a* **corona**; *and also without buccal tactile setæ. It also becomes attenuated in front ; so that the buccal aperture comes to be situated at the apex of a small cone.*

PARASEISON PROBOSCIDEUS, *Plate* (192).

SP. CH. *Head without any trace of* **corona**, *without tactile setæ at the mouth, but with a small proboscidiform eversion of the skin, situated above the buccal aperture, which serves as a tactile organ. Rare.*
Length, ₃½₄ inch.

PARASEISON CILIATUS, *Plate* (192).

SP. CII. *Assists in the transition to the genus* SEISON, *inasmuch as the* **corona** *is developed as in that genus ; and further there are, on the ventral surface, two longitudinal streaks composed of numerous parallel muscular fibres. Not uncommon.*
Length. About ₂½₃ inch.

Genus SACCOBDELLA, *Van Beneden and Hesse* (162).

SACCOBDELLA NEBALIÆ, *Van Beneden and Hesse* (162),

The abdomen terminates in two pedunculate sucking discs. Neck composed of five segments of about equal length. Foot of four rings. Buccal aperture on the lower surface of the head, not far from the anterior margin. The intestine is said to traverse the whole body in the median line. Colour of the body a very light blue. The ova possess a small stalk, and several of them may be united to form a bush-like group. In the North Sea.
Length. From ₁½₂ to ½ inch.
M. A. F. Marion (114) says that *Nebalia Straussii* lives shut up, in July and August, in the voluminous mass of the rudimentary capsules of *Murex brandaris* ; and that *Saccobdella* adheres to the foliated branchial feet of the young *Nebaliæ*, when they are in the " poche incubatrice " under their mother's carapace.

Paraseison, according to Dr. L. Plate, attaches itself, by preference, to the branchial laminæ of *Nebalia*, but also creeps about on all other regions of the body. It attaches itself by the adhesive secretion of its foot-glands ; and, as there are not unfrequently several ova lying together (in one case there were eleven) in different stages of develop-

ment, it is probable that the adult animal remains for a long time in one place. Sometimes it seeks its nourishment—vegetable detritus and decomposed particles of *Nebalia's*
eggs—by bending its body nearly at a right-angle and feeling about with its head,
stretching its swan-like neck in all directions, and every moment retracting it completely
into the trunk.[1]

MASTIGOCERCA CORNUTA, Eyferth (Pl. XXXIII. fig. 21).

Monocerca cornuta . . . . Eyferth (46).

SP. CII. **Body** *a long cone, with a long very low dorsal ridge, continuous with the
frontal spine ; front beset with five projecting* **spines** ; **toe** *nearly as long as the lorica ;
no* **sub-styles.**

There is one spine continuing the dorsal ridge or groin beyond the edge of the lorica ;
this is the longest of the five. Opposite to it, from the ventral edge, project a pair of
about half the size ; and there is also on each side another short spine, dividing the
space between the dorsal and ventral spines. Herr Eyferth adds that the long **toe** is
slightly bent downwards, so that the dorsal spine, dorsal ridge, and toe together form a
curve : a curve, however, which his figure hardly shows.

Length. Including the toe, $\frac{1}{70}$ inch.

MASTIGOCERCA IERNIS, Gosse (171), (Pl. XXXI. fig. 26).

[SP. CII. **Body** *long-oval ; a long dorsal* **ridge** *throughout, rising abruptly with an
oblique edge in front ;* **toe** *not so long as lorica ;* **sub-styles** *two, unequal, the chief one
about one-third as long as the toe, remote from it at the base.*

This species has much resemblance to *M. scipio* ; but the regular form of the lorica
and that of its ridge, and the origination of the toe and of the main sub-style, on *opposite* sides of the foot-bulb, so as to be remote from each other, seem sufficient peculiarities to warrant its distinctness.

Several examples have occurred in *Utricularia vulgaris*, sent me by Mr. W. R. Hood
from a lough in the heart of Ireland. Most of these were dead, mere empty loricæ,
affording excellent opportunities for precise observation and delineation ; others were
alive and active. I subsequently found it in water from Cannock Chase, sent by Mr.
Bolton. The distinctive characters noted above were conspicuous in all : as also in some
vigorous examples from Perthshire. In these the extremities of the jaws were occasionally protruded. I detected, moreover, on the front, three tubercles (one central and two
lateral), which seemed fleshy, extensile, and retractile.

Length (entire), $\frac{1}{80}$ inch. **Habitat.** Lacustrine. P.II.G.]

MASTIGOCERCA BICRISTATA, Gosse (169), (Pl. XXXI. fig. 27).

[SP. CII. *Two equal sub-parallel* **carinæ,** *running nearly the whole length of the
dorsum.*

Discovered near Dundee by Mr. Hood, who sent me from time to time many examples.
It has a general likeness to *M. carinata,* but is much larger. The double carina confirms the conjecture that the asymmetry of that and other species is due to unequal
development.

The **carinæ** are thick at their base, and sharp at their edge, so that the furrow is
sharp at the bottom, and has sloping sides.

Length, $\frac{1}{50}$ inch, of which the toe is nearly half. **Habitat.** Dundee (J.II.). P.II.G.]

MONOCERCA VALGA, *Ehrenberg* (12), is probably a male Rotiferon.

---

[1] The whole of the above account of the *Scisonidæ* has been taken from a translation of the
Mittheilungen aus der Zoologischen Station zu Neapel, Bd. vii. pp. 234-263, published in the *Annals
and Magazine of Natural History*, No. vii. July 1888.

STEPHANOPS CIRRATUS, *Ehrenberg* (12), (Pl. XXXIII. fig. 25).

SP. CH. **Lorica** *armed behind with two spines.*

Ehrenberg merely notices the presence of the mastax, alimentary canal, gastric glands, ovary, contractile vesicle, lateral canals, and two red, frontal eyes.

Müller's very characteristic figure (published 1773) of this Rotiferon is given in outline in Pl. B. fig. 20.

Length, $\frac{1}{210}$ inch. **Habitat.** Near Copenhagen, and Berlin.

STEPHANOPS TRIPUS,[1] *Lord* (112), (Pl. XXXIII. fig. 24).

SP. CH. **Body** *pyriform behind, cylindrical and obliquely truncate in front, with a curved tapering dorsal* **spine** *about the length of the head and trunk;* **foot** *jointless, with two toes, and a short dorsal* **process** *;* **eyes** *absent.*

Mr. Lord, who discovered this species in 1884, gives (*loc. cit.*) the following account of it. It is obliquely truncate in front; anteriorly cylindrical for about ½ of its length; enlarging thence to about the middle of the body, whence it gradually decreases to the base of the foot : here it is suddenly diminished to a short tapering foot, with two **toes**, and a dorsal **process** springing almost from between them. The toes are about the length of the foot. There are no **eyes**, and the frontal hood, seen sidewise, looks like a hook. The cilia are in bundles ; and a long, tapering **spine** springs from the centre of the dorsal region : the internal organs are difficult to make out : rare.

Length. Not recorded. **Habitat.** A ditch containing *Anacharis* (Lord).

STEPHANOPS LEYDIGII, *Zacharias* (201).

SP. CH. **Body** *spindle-shaped ;* **dorsal spine** *exceeding the animal's total length ;* **foot** *with two joints, but without dorsal* **process** *;* **eyes** *two, minute.*

Dr. Zacharias, in his account of *Leydigii*, seems to incline to the opinion that it is identical with *tripus*. There are, however, several points of difference. *Leydigii* has no dorsal process at the end of the foot, above the toes : and its large dorsal spine is as long as the whole animal, while that of *tripus* is not as long as the head and trunk. Moreover *Leydigii* tapers, from the middle of the body, towards both extremities; and is, especially in front, not nearly so bulky an animal. Besides *tripus* is said to have no eyes, while *Leydigii* has two minute red eye-specks : though it is possible, of course, that these may have been overlooked.

Length, $\frac{1}{17}$ inch. **Habitat.** Marsh-water (Zacharias).

STEPHANOPS STYLATUS, *Milne* (186), (Pl. XXXIII. fig. 27).

SP. CH. **Lorica** *flattened ; its oval dorsal surface prolonged forward into a spoon-shaped hood, backward to the middle of the foot, and there rounded off without* **spines** *;* **foot** *long, ending in two long, decurved, and divergent* **toes.**

The lorica is transparent, and rather tough than hard. The **corona** is nearly level with the ventral surface. It has a few small cilia round the oral opening, in front of which is a central spoon of uncinate styles. On either side of these a very strong uncinate one is placed, and at their roots a few smaller ones. These *styles* seem to be ambulatory. From each side of the **head** proceeds backwards and outwards a very long straight style of a soft and flexible character, but not vibratile. Near the bases of these styles are two fairly large green nodules, which can be isolated. The **brain-mass** is occipital. The **mastax** has small trophi somewhat like those of *Notops clavulatus*. The

---

[1] Mr. Lord did not name this *Stephanops*; so I have given it a specific title from the tripod-like ending of the foot.

contractile vesicle is large, and appears double. When it contracts, its convoluted corded surface seems to go down by the run, in two divisions, right and left of the cloaca. This Rotifcron is very lively, and flits about in the most graceful way, running up the moss in search of food by means of its uncini (Milne, *loc. cit.*).

Length, $\frac{1}{130}$ inch. **Habitat.** Near Glasgow (Milne).

STEPHANOPS OVALIS, *Schmarda* (135). See note 1, Sup‘. p. 8.

DIASCHIZA ACRONOTA, *Gosse* (171), (Pl. XXXI. fig. 29).

[SP. CH. **Lorica** *much elevated, heart-shaped in lateral outline ; the* **dorsal cleft** *very manifest ;* **head** *globose, prominent ;* **foot** *thick ;* **toes** *stout, long, nearly straight, tapering ;* **eye** *occipital, pale, very large.*

This very remarkable form is another novelty yielded by the mill-stream at Kingskerswell. It seems a very distinct and interesting species ; though known, as yet, only by a single dead specimen, in which the eye and the trophi remained in position. The **eye** is a remarkable feature, from its great size, irregular shape, and pale hue. It occupies nearly half the vertical depth of the body, of a very pale salmon-red. In all these points it resembles the organ in *D. pœta.* The **mastax** is small ; the toes have a backward curve, so slight as to be scarcely perceptible.

Length, $\frac{1}{140}$ inch. **Habitat.** Kingskerswell, lacustrine. P.II.G.]

DIASCHIZA FRETALIS, *Gosse* (171), (Pl. XXXI. fig. 28).

[SP. CH. **Lorica** *pyriform in outline, viewed dorsally ; gibbous laterally ; each plate cut off obliquely behind, and somewhat excavate ;* **belly** *nearly flat ;* **toes** *long, blade-shaped, regularly decurved, acute ;* **head** *furnished with a beak-like projection.*

This form comes very near to *D. rhamphigera*, but the oblique excavation of each of the dorsal lorica-plates is much more distinct, the frontal beak is more slender, nearly evanescent, and does not appear to be a prolongation of the trophi, which, moreover, are somewhat diversely shaped. There is a red **eye** on the inner surface of the brain, which I did not perceive in *D. rhamphigera* ; and, above all, it is marine.

Only a single specimen has been observed, and that *dead* ; but so recently as to leave the internal organs and viscera well-defined, and *in situ.* It was from a tide-pool at Invergowric. Both species, if they are distinct, require further study.

Length, $\frac{1}{135}$ inch. **Habitat.** Marine. P.H.G.]

DIASCHIZA GLOBATA, *Gosse* (170), (Pl. XXXI. fig. 30).

[SP. CH. **Body** *sub-pyriform, becoming globose in contraction ; front round, girded by a prominent ring ;* **lorica** *dorsally cleft by a wide, but shallow furrow, whose edges rise to slight ridges ;* **foot** *stout ;* **toes** *slender, produced, acute, slightly decurved.*

The shallow dorsal cleft, having a V-shaped section, is well seen, as the creature crawls about the weeds, the edges turned up slightly ; while the sides of the lorica end ventrally in straight lines, produced behind into small obtuse points. The integument appears sometimes quite flexible. The bluff rounded **head**, clothed with simple cilia, is surrounded by a prominent ring or collar, not always observable. An occipital **brain** seems destitute of any eye-spot. The toes are delicately attenuated to long points, which, *more generis*, are often thrown back, though the points are decurved.

The little animal is active and restless, moderately swift in swimming, with frequent augmentations of speed, sudden and sustained. It soon dies in a *live-box* ; and, in dying, usually contracts itself into a globular form. Sometimes it spins swiftly round and round, in a circle of which the toe-tips are the centre. I have examined some eight or ten specimens, all in water sent by Mr. Hood from his aquarium at Dundee.

Length, $\frac{1}{200}$ inch. **Habitat.** Dundee, lacustrine. P.H.G.]

Diaschiza (?) cupha, *Gosse* (169), (Pl. XXXI. fig. 31).

[SP. CII.   *Much compressed ; dorsum squarely gibbous ; foot short, scarcely protruding ;* toes *long, blade-shaped, slightly recurved, with claws abruptly shouldered.*

This hunchbacked form needs fuller examination.   I describe it from a single example, just dead but not decomposed, in water sent from Birmingham.   The depth, compared with the width, of the animal is remarkable.   The **trophi** are very long, but ill-defined ; in the occiput is a short **brain**, carrying a flat, lens-shaped red **eye** on its inner surface.   The peculiar shape of the **toes** is shown at fig. 31, *b*.   I affix a mark of doubt to the *generic* position, because I could not be *quite* sure of the dorsal cleft.

Length, $\frac{1}{71}$ inch.   **Habitat.** Birmingham, lacustrine.   P.H.G.]

Diaschiza (?) ramphigera, *Gosse* (169), (Pl. XXXI. fig. 82).

[SP. CII.   **Lorica** *elliptical in outline, viewed dorsally ; highly gibbous, viewed laterally ;* **venter** *flat ;* toes *stout, long, decurved ;* **trophi** *projecting in form of a bird's beak.*

The **front** terminates in an acute hooked beak, which is found to be the extremity of the trophi, and apparently of the incus protruded.   The whole **manducatory** apparatus is of unusual dimensions, especially the fulcrum of the incus.   (Fig. 32, *b*, represents the trophi seen dorsally ; *c*, laterally.)   I have not distinctly seen the **dorsal cleft** ; but the line which passes along the back, at some distance from the edge, I presume to indicate the bottom of such a cleft ; if it is not the base of a high carina.   Two examples occurred together in water from one of my window tanks.

Length, $\frac{1}{113}$ inch.   **Habitat.** Lacustrine.   P.H.G.]

Salpina ventralis, *Ehrenberg* (42), (Pl. XXXIII. fig. 29).

SP. CII.   *Occipital spines wanting ;* **pectoral** *pair very short ;* **lumbar spine** *short, decurved ;* **alvine** *pair longer than the lumbar, straight ; the* **lorica** *with a stippled collar in front.*

This species closely resembles Mr. Gosse's *macracantha* ; but differs from it in having a rather decurved **lumbar** spine instead of a straight one ; in its alvine spines being proportionally longer ; and in having a stippled collar on its lorica surface, which *macracantha* lacks.   It is (according to Ehr.) considerably smaller.

Length (of lorica), $\frac{1}{120}$ inch.   **Habitat.** Near Berlin.

Salpina bicarinata, *Ehrenberg* (42), (Pl. XXXIII. fig. 30).

SP. CII.   **Lorica** *smooth, four* **processes** *in front, three small ones behind,* **alvine** *pair the smaller.*

Very like *mucronata*, only all the **spines** are shorter ; and the gaps between the **pectoral** and **alvine** are different.   The gap between the pectoral pair is nearly straight with a slight central incision, while the corresponding gap in *mucronata* is very deep.

Length, $\frac{1}{210}$ inch.   **Habitat.** Near Berlin.

Salpina polyodonta, *Schmarda* (185), (Pl. XXXIII. fig. 28).

SP. CII.   **Body** *sub-triquetrous ;* **pectoral** spines *two-pointed ; the middle* **hind** spine *blunter than the* alvine.   *Two rows of* **teeth** *in each uncus.*

This *Salpina* has a lorica differing from that of *brevispina* only in the **pectoral** spines.   As will be seen from the figure, each pectoral projection is double-cornered, unlike any other *Salpina.*   Schmarda credits the animal with two rows of teeth in each uncus ; I think that this must be an error.

Length.   About $\frac{1}{100}$ inch.   **Habitat.** St. Jago, Chili.

SALPINA MARINA, *Gosse* (109), (Pl. XXXI. fig. 33).

[SP. CH. **Occipital** *spines two, procurved;* **pectoral** *two, short;* **lumbar** *spine short, deep;* **alvines** *stout, separated from the lumbar by an angular sulcus.*

This large species was taken in a tide-pool in the Firth of Tay; the first *Salpina* found in the sea. Its anterior armature is that of *S. mucronata*, but the posterior is peculiar, in that the alvines are stout, nearly straight spines, and that the sinus which divides each from the lumbar point is not rounded, but makes two sides of a rhomboid, with definite angles. The specimen was dead when I found it.

Length (of lorica from points to points), $\frac{1}{3}\frac{}{0}$ inch. **Habitat.** Marine. P.H.G.]

SALPINA REDUNCA, *Ehrenberg* (42). This is, I think, *S. brevispina.* The only differ-ence is, that its lorica is said to be smooth in front instead of being stippled.

SALPINA AFFINIS, *Herrick* (175). Very like *mucronata*, but with longer occipital and alvine spines.

EUCHLANIS CONICA, *Schmarda* (185), (Pl. XXXIII. fig. 34).

SP. CH. **Lorica** *conical; dorsal occipital edge concave, semi-elliptical; hind dorsal edge with a semicircular notch; three* **teeth** *in each malleus.*

This curious *Euchlanis* adds to the attraction of its unusual shape, **trophi** tinted brown, and a reddish-brown **ovary.** It has a transversely oval red **eye**, and two long **toes**; but no setæ on its **foot.** Schmarda says nothing about the ventral plate, but the figure seems to show a portion of its margin well within that of the dorsal one: neither does he say if the dorsal plate is arched or depressed.

Length (to end of foot), $\frac{1}{85}$ inch. **Habitat.** Fresh-water, near San Juan del Norte, Central America (Schm.).

EUCHLANIS OROPHA, *Gosse* (109), (Pl. XXXI. fig. 34).

[SP. CH. **Lorica** *roof-shaped with sloping sides, but not rising to a ridge, yet cleft for a short distance behind, between two descending extremities.* **Ventral plate** *flat, thin, much smaller in its whole outline than the dorsal;* **foot** *with a single seta or none;* **toes** *thin, blade-shaped.*

This is a noble species, and not uncommon. The posterior fourth of the ovate lorica seems as if pinched-in, and the dorsal edge *of this portion* becomes a low double carina. In fig. *b*, the inner outline is that of this portion, the outer outline represents a trans-verse section through the highest point in figure 34 *a*.

Length, $\frac{1}{15}$ inch. **Habitat.** Lacustrine. P.H.G.]

EUCHLANIS PANNONICA, *Bartsch* (8), (Pl. XXXIII. 33).

SP. CH. **Lorica** *ovately oblong, large;* **foot** *long, without setæ;* **toes** *very short.*

Dr. Bartsch has unfortunately given the rest of his description of this species in Hungarian; but his figure shows a very deep **gap** at the posterior end of the dorsal plate. This character, along with the large **foot** and very short **toes**, entitle *pannonica* to be considered a distinct species.

Length, $\frac{1}{100}$ inch. **Habitat.** Hungary (Bartsch).

E. HYALINA, *Leydig* (110). This name has been given by Leydig to a variety of *E. tri-quetra*, conspicuous for its general lack of colour, its less lofty dorsal ridge, and the notching of the hinder end of the nervous ganglion. The first of these distinctions is probably a temporary one, and the last is to be seen occasionally in other species; I have met with it, for instance, in *pyriformis*. The second, however, makes me think that Leydig's *hyalina* may possibly be the variety of *triquetra* that I have drawn in Pl. XXIII. fig. 4; for, since the publication of vols. i. and ii., Mr. C. Rousselet has sent me some specimens of a fine *Euchlanis* most closely resembling Ehrenberg's drawings of *triquetra*, and differing from mine in having its ventral plate perfectly flat, and apparently attached closely to the dorsal plate. Certainly it had no flanges bent down like those given in fig. 4 c, and its dorsal ridge was decidedly higher.

E. WEISSEI, *Eichwald* (167), (Pl. XXXIII. fig. 35). Eichwald describes the lorica as longer than that of *dilatata*, narrower in front and broader behind. His figure, which I have copied, makes the lorica a narrow truncated oval, the anterior end of which is bounded by a shallow circular arc, and the posterior end hollowed into a deep sinus. The foot has four joints, and very long tapering toes ; the eye is dark red and nearly triangular. Both description and figure are very imperfect.

Habitat. Ditches at Reval.

E. (?) LYNCEUS, *Ehrenberg* (42), (Pl. XXXIII. fig. 32). SP. CII. "Lorica *oval*, *swollen, enwrapping the body, deeply furrowed, with two anterior spines.*" Ehrenberg says that *lynceus*, though very like the crustacean after which he has named it, is an unmistakable Rotiferon : having (apparently) single-toothed jaws, short œsophagus, a thick and almost circular stomach, with two gastric glands, an obvious antenna lying between the spines, a red cervical eye, and a long forked foot. He further notices that there is, at the anterior end of the dorsal surface, a detached portion of the lorica, which is flattish and triangular, and which bears the two spines on its front edge. Ehrenberg says that the lorica is cleft down the whole length of its ventral surface ; and his figure shows a wide gap between its edges.

If the lorica has been rightly described and figured, it would be difficult to say where this creature should be placed ; but as Ehrenberg has made mistakes on this very point in the *Euchlanidæ*, it will be as well to leave the name unaltered till the animal has been met with again, and thoroughly studied. It is very unlikely to prove to be a *Euchlanis*.

Length, $_2|_6$ *inch.* **Habitat.** Near Berlin.

E. (?) BICARINATA, *Perty* (124), (Pl. XXXIII. fig. 31). The lorica of this Rotiferon, according to Perty, covers only the back and sides of the body, and is absent from a central strip of the ventral surface.[1] It is moderately broad in the middle, diminishing towards either end, truncate and spineless in front, and with its hinder portion like that of a *Salpina*, whose alvine processes had been rounded off. Down the back run two long parallel ridges, which, in Perty's dorsal and side views, are precisely those of a *Salpina*. The foot is remarkable for the great length of its middle joint, and the shortness of the last joint and toes. The drawing of the corona is incomprehensible, and that of the internal structure little better. Under these circumstances it is impossible to decide to what genus the animal really belongs.

Length (total), $_7|_8$ inch. **Habitat.** Near Bern.

E. CORNUTA, *Dujardin* (40)=*Monostyla cornuta* (vol. ii. p. 98).

E. OVALIS, *Dujardin* (40)=*E. macrura* (vol. ii. p. 91).

E. HIPPOSIDEROS, *Gosse* (54). Cancelled by Mr. Gosse.

E. EMARGINATA, *Eichwald* (167)= *Cathypna luna* (vol. ii. p. 94).

E. BRACHYDACTYLA and E. TETRAODON, *Schmarda* (134, 135). See note 1, Sup[t], p. 8.

E. AMPULLIFORMIS, *Herrick* (175). Somewhat flask-shaped ; dorsal plate carinate ; ventral plate with a cordate posterior opening. Foot four-jointed ; toes half the length of the lorica. Figure and description imperfect.

APODOIDES STYGIUS, *Joseph* (96). Dr. G. Joseph discovered this Rotiferon, for which he has formed a new genus, in the stalactite caves of Krainer.

---

[1] See note, vol. ii. p. 89.

It much resembles a *Euchlanis* ; the **lorica** is in two plates, the dorsal, arched and expanded at the sides, which are bent sharply back underneath. The ventral plate is flat, and fills up the gap between the bent-back edges of the dorsal plate. In front, and behind, the lorica is cut away by a half-moon-shaped scollop, and is prolonged at the extremities of each semicircular edge into spines, of which the posterior pair is the longer. The foot is four-jointed, and bifurcate. There are no **eyes** ; but, on the spots where they should be, are two small hollow protuberances, from which rise two long movable antennæ, with bristle-like ends, stretching forward beyond the corona. Two smaller bristles spring from the spot which in *Euchlanis* bears a spur-like antenna. Dr. Joseph is of opinion that the young **male** and **female** are precisely alike in structure; but that the male gradually loses the whole of the digestive tract, as it approaches maturity. His account leaves it doubtful whether he is describing a succession of changes that he has watched in the same individual, or whether he is detailing inferences that he has drawn from various individuals observed at different times. Dr. Joseph gives no figure of the animal.

Length, $\frac{1}{30}$ inch.

Genus DAPIDIA, *Gosse* (170).

GEN. CII. *A genus of the* Euchlanidæ, *whose* **ventral plate** *is wanting ; the turned-in lateral edges of the* **dorsal plate** *being united only by a flexible and expansible skin.*

DAPIDIA STROMA, *Gosse* (170), (Pl. XXXI., fig. 85).

[SP. CII. *Outline ovate,* **dorsum** *high, rounded ;* **lorica** *much exceeding the viscera in width, and turned in beneath with straight margins ;* **viscera** *protected exclusively by membrane.*

Dr. Hudson (vol. ii. p. 93) has alluded to my opinion that certain species of *Euchlanis* are generically separable by the character of wanting a ventral plate ; the lateral edges of the lorica, which turn in beneath, being united only by flexible and expansible skin. My esteemed colleague differs from me ; and, on a matter so exceedingly delicate and difficult to determine, I may be in the wrong. But I am not convinced ; and I hope it is not inconsistent with modesty or friendship to record my own judgment.[1] The *species*, I think, is undescribed, whatever its generic place.

The lorica is shaped (if I may use so homely a comparison) like a boat turned bottom up, her bows cut off sharp, her gunwale curved-in, and no keel. Suppose the cavity of the boat to be loaded, *half-way up*, with goods [the viscera], and a tarpaulin [the common skin] to be spread over all, but higher in the middle than at the sides ; the head-mass, of living fleshy organs, to be thrust out at the truncate and open bow, filling it ; and the foot and toes to represent the rudder ;—a fair idea will be conceived of this fine form. There are no foot-setæ.

It may easily be supposed to possess a ventral plate. But what looks like one, on a (nearly) lateral view, is the edge of the farther incurved side of the lorica ; when viewed *from behind*, there is no lateral infold or sinus running longitudinally. I have seen numerous examples.

Length, $\frac{1}{75}$ inch. **Habitat.** Lacustrine. P.II.G.]

CATHYPNA DIOMIS, *Gosse* (170), (Pl. XXXI. fig. 88).

[SP. CII. *Generally like* C. luna, *but* **lorica** *much elevated behind, and ending there abruptly ; followed by a wide hemispheric joint ;* **toes** *slightly blade-shaped ;* **claw** *two-shouldered, short, recurved.*

A rather remarkable little form. The lorica, broadly ovate, is unusually arched, and abruptly truncate just behind its greatest elevation ; whence another wide rounded plate

---

[1] It was with reference to *Euchlanis deflexa* that I differed from Mr. Gosse ; I have not seen *Dapidia stroma*.

descends, as if to make the lorica two-jointed. The **foot** narrow, but a little widened at its end, just protrudes from under this plate, and bears the toes, jointed to it with small round condyles. They are almost rod-shaped, but there is a hardly perceptible curvature of their lateral margins. But the most noteworthy feature is that *both* the lateral margins of each toe are abruptly shouldered; and the little claw-like remainder has the acute tip recurved. The **mallei** are long, strongly elbowed, and unusually slender. An **eye**, of moderate size, richly coloured, lies far down in the occiput. The dorsal plate is coarsely tessellated, as in *C. rusticula*. Several specimens have occurred in water sent to me by Mr. Hood, from Black Loch, near Dundee.

Length (of lorica), $\frac{1}{210}$ inch; (total) $\frac{1}{130}$ inch. **Habitat.** Lacustrine. P.H.G.]

CATHYPNA LATIFRONS, *Gosse* (170), (Pl. XXXI. fig. 37).

[SP. CH. **Lorica** *broadly ovate, the frontal edges little diminished, both straight; the occipital much wider than the pectoral;* **toes** *broadly blade-shaped, much produced, not shouldered.*

Another of the rarities of the prolific Black Loch. The outline is that of *C. rusticula*, if we suppose the anterior fourth of the lorica to be cut off transversely. But the ventral plate is less in area, *all round*, than the dorsal, especially forward, narrowing more rapidly, and terminating lower down. There is a considerable rounded boss behind, as in both the preceding, below (or within) which are the foot-joints, but not protruded. The **toes** have the inner edge straight, and the outer *much* outcurved; so that, when they are held in contact (as they usually are), the pair present an outline widely fusiform. Then the points are drawn out to great length and tenuity, with an effect very peculiar. The front of the lorica forms two stiff lateral points; within which the margins, both occipital and pectoral, seem to be thinned-off to very delicate membranes, so as to be capable of extension and retraction. When closed, the occipital edge is, I think, straight from point to point, and concave inward. Then the pectoral edge is appressed to the concave dorsal surface (*but at a lower*, i.e. *a hinder, level*); and that so close as to be indistinguishable from it, even by most careful focusing with high powers. The internal organs seem normal.

Length (of lorica), $\frac{1}{210}$ inch. **Habitat.** Lacustrine.

CATHYPNA UNGULATA, *Gosse* (170), (Pl. XXXI. fig. 36).

[SP. CH. *Generally like* C. luna, *but occipital edge of lorica nearly straight; pectoral edge indented in the middle;* **toe** *rod-shaped, straight, very slender;* **claw** *one-shouldered, one-third of toe's length.*

This is more than twice as large as *C. luna*. Moreover, the frontal edges of the lorica are nearly *straight*, between very slight lateral points, and *alike*, save that the line of the pectoral edge (fig. 36, *b*) descends from each point to a medial angle, just perceptible. Then, the hind extremity of the dorsal plate allows the partial emission of a great protuberant shelly boss, as in *Monostyla bulla*, behind and beneath which is the globose foot-bulb. Again, the rod-like **toes** are even straighter and slenderer than in *luna*, and the claws are much longer in proportion. Parallel-edged to two-thirds of their length, a right-angled shoulder, on the outer side, reduces the width by one-half; and the remainder (the claw) tapers to a long-drawn acute point (*d*). When rotating, the truncate front is three-lobed, much as in *luna*; but there is seen beyond and above this a very subtile clear glassy **hood**, having a rondo-conic outline, protrusile and retractile.

Length (total), $\frac{1}{45}$ inch. **Habitat.** Woolston pond. P.H.G.]

DISTYLA HORNEMANNI, *Ehrenberg* (Pl. XXXIII. fig. 37).

Euchlanis Hornemanni . . . . . Ehrenberg (42).

SP. CH. **Lorica** *smooth, short, semi-orbicular, broadly truncated in front, and without lateral points; the former part of the body soft, flexible, and much elongated;*

capable of being retracted within the lorica ; **brain** *long, and cylindrical ;* **foot** *very short ;* **toes** *straight, ending in small, sharp, unshouldered claws.*

The above characteristics, which I have taken from Ehrenberg's figure and description, remove this animal from the genus *Euchlanis* to that of *Distyla.* Ehrenberg says that, when fully extended, it looks like a *Notommata.* The **mastax** is oval ; the œsophagus very short ; the **stomach** simple ; the **gastric glands** spherical ; the **brain** long and cylindrical, with a red **eye** on its hinder end.

Length, $\frac{1}{137}$ to $\frac{1}{110}$ inch. **Habitat.** Near Copenhagen (Ehr.).

DISTYLA LUDWIGII, *Eckstein* (41), (Pl. XXXIII. fig. 36).

SP. CII. **Lorica** *ovate, drawn out into a point behind, and slightly hollowed out in front, between two sharp points ; dorsal plate somewhat swollen, tesselated, scabrous ; ventral plate flat ;* **toes** *long, scythe-shaped, wide apart at the base ;* **claws** *not shouldered, short ;* **brain** *tri-lobed.*

The fore part of the body is soft and flexible, and of the shape of a truncate cone. The **corona** is feebly developed. The **brain** has one long central lobe, bearing at its hinder end a red **eye** just above the mastax ; and two shorter club-shaped lobes, each carrying, on the inner side of its hinder end, a clear cell, coloured red on the inner border. The small upper ends of these two lobes terminate on the corona, in two minute red points.[1]

Four **vibratile tags** are seen on each side (with the lateral canals), in a rather advanced position. The rest of the organisation is normal.

The creature has a habit of constantly twitching its œsophagus from side to side. It generally carries its toes wide apart, but sometimes draws them together and bends them up to the ventral surface.

Length, $\frac{1}{100}$ inch. **Habitat.** Near Giessen (Eckstein).

DISTYLA STRIATA, *Gosse* (169), (Pl. XXXI. fig. 40).

[SP. CII. **Lorica** *as in D. Gissensis, but covered with longitudinal sulci ; the front margin projecting in two lateral points (which, however, are lost in the protrusion of the head, by the evolution of flexible membrane) ;* **toes** *slender, straight, more than half as long as lorica, pointed, not shouldered.*

The lateral infold is narrow and nearly closed. The dorsal sulci are about eight in number, slender and superficial : foot a long large bulb, not divisible into joints ; **toes** long, nearly straight, rods. The dorsal surface is corrugated, besides the sulci ; there is a minute **eye**, difficult of detection. Two examples occurred in water sent me by Dr. F. Collins from the pool at Sandhurst Military College.

Length, $\frac{1}{130}$ inch. **Habitat.** Lacustrine. P.H.G.]

DISTYLA LIPARA, *Gosse* (171), (Pl. XXXI. fig. 39).

[SP. CII. **Lorica** *skin-like, flexible, plicate : body flask-shaped, soft and very plump, not pointed behind :* **toes** *large, blade-shaped, not shouldered :* **brain** *simple ;* **eye** *minute, occipital.*

This differs, at sight, from its known congeners by its round, manifestly soft, body, properly egg-shaped, specially in its hind parts, scarcely at all flattened, and destitute of the usual inangulation ; the edges of the dorsal and ventral plates approaching close in the middle, and diverging at both extremities, so that the rounded surface is scarcely broken. The soft integument is constantly thrown into deep irregular plicæ, which do not appear to be permanent. A great **foot** bears, on a condyliform joint, two toes which are widely blade-shaped, longer than the mastax, acute, but not in the least shouldered

---

[1] See note, vol. ii. p. 37. Both Mr. Gosse and myself have failed to see many of Herr Eckstein's red spots.

at the tips. They are habitually thrown up under the belly. The **eye** is minute, pale-red, occipital. The **trophi** are normal, long, and capable of being brought to the very front, where they work vigorously. The whole head is protrusile, and very mobile.

The entire animal is transparent and nearly colourless ; but the numerous folds and corrugations impart an appearance of a blue-black tinge to the body. The form and outline are subject to slight but continual changes, contracting and expanding. The animal is lithe and active, but not locomotive. A single specimen has occurred in water from Sutton Park ditch, Birmingham, in the orange-coloured sediment which abounds with fine Desmidieæ.

Length (of lorica), $\frac{1}{200}$ inch ; (total) $\frac{1}{137}$ inch. **Habitat.** Sutton Park. P.H.G.]

D. MINNESOTENSIS ; D. OHIOENSIS, *Herrick* (175). Insufficiently described. The latter is said to have a quadrate plate projecting over the base of the foot.

MONOSTYLA MOLLIS, *Gosse* (170), (Pl. XXXI. fig. 41).

[SP. CH. **Body** *oblong, sub-cylindric, clothed with a soft, flexible, corrugated skin, instead of a lorica ;* **toe** *rod-shaped, short, thick ;* **claw** *obscurely two-shouldered.*

I venture to claim specific rank for this form, which has the same relation to *Monostyla* as *D. flexilis* has to *Distyla* and *Cathypna*. That both are immature conditions would be a natural conclusion, but that, so far as my experience goes, all Loricate Rotifera are hatched with the lorica already developed. And that such is the case with *Monostyla* in particular, the following note will show. The facts, apart from their relation to this question, may be of interest.

In August 1885, an egg of *M. cornuta*, in my live-box, displayed the young moving vigorously within the hyaline egg-shell, slowly revolving. The lorica was already well-defined, evidently without folds, though expansile in retraction, distinctly broad oval in outline, smooth and rotund when viewed lengthwise. The imprisoned animal grew much larger, so that it almost filled the long diameter of the shell, but not nearly its short diameter. Its length was now $\frac{1}{100}$ inch.

After I had watched for about an hour, during which its restless motions had nearly ceased, the frontal cilia were seen vibrating at the very edge, and in a moment more *outside* the edge, of the shell. For an instant it recoiled ; but returned again and again to the effort, at each time protruding more and more. At length it pushed fully half out, then hung a moment, as if exhausted. Now another vigorous lashing of the cilia, and out it is bodily, yet still adhering to the shell by the glutinous toe-point, whereby it now drags the shell hither and thither. At last it is quite free, evidently ovate, stiff and smooth, as the normal adult.

These facts, which were recorded during the actual process, seem sufficient to show that, in this Family at least, the chitinous consolidation of the lorica is attained before birth. And the corollary follows, that, in *D. flexilis* and *M. mollis* we have examples of illoricate condition in a loricate family, analogous to *Mastigocerca stylata* in the *Rattulidæ*.

I have examined many specimens from various waters. In one case the animal contracted to a cordiform outline, as if possessing a lorica, which yet was very membranous. When eagerly chewing, not only the **mallei** worked, but a pair of additional horn-like pieces, well in front of the mastax. A very small and indistinct red **eye** is near the occipital extremity of the brain.

Length, $\frac{1}{250}$ to $\frac{1}{300}$ inch. **Habitat.** Lacustrine. P.H.G.]

MONOSTYLA CLOSTEROCERCA, *Schmarda* (195), (Pl. XXXIV. fig. 7).

SP. CII. **Lorica** *depressed, obtusely toothed in front ;* **eye** *very small and round ;* **jaws** *triangular ;* **foot** *spindle-shaped.*

The **lorica** is oval with its anterior portion excised so as to give it a shallow circular margin. The spindle-shaped **foot** ends in a tapering, finely pointed, claw, and is the really characteristic point in the animal's shape. Its " triangular " teeth are, I fear, due to imperfect observation. No further details are given.

Length, $_2\frac{1}{10}$ **inch. Habitat.** Freshwater, Quito (Schmarda).

M. MACROGNATHA and M. OÖPHTHALMA, *Schmarda* (185). See note 1, Sup¹, p. 8.

COLURUS DUMNONIUS, *Gosse* (169), (Pl. XXXI. fig. 44).

[SP. CII. **Lorica** *in dorsal aspect a very broad oval, produced behind into two rather short points, separated by a wide but shallow sinus; the ventral line deepens in the middle; the ventral cleft extends around the front to the occiput;* **foot** *robust, with two moderately stout, separable toes.*

Three examples I have seen at different times among fine conferva, much studded with *Licmophoreæ*, from tide-pools at Paignton, near Torquay. One of these had the sides much more parallel than the other. A large pale red **eye** is conspicuous. All had the habit of pivoting on the toe-tips, jerking and posturing.

Length, $_2\frac{1}{50}$ inch. **Habitat.** Marine; Paignton. P.H.G.]

COLURUS DICENTRUS, *Gosse* (169), (Pl. XXXI. fig. 42).

[SP. CII. **Lorica** *ovato-fusiform; body ending behind in a minute tail of two hooks adnate at their base;* **foot** *stout; toes long, very slender, more or less decurved throughout.*

I have examined nearly a score of individuals, and am satisfied that this is a true species, in which the peculiar termination of the body (shown enlarged in fig. *b*) is constant, thus differing from *C. amblytelus* and *C. grallator*. The **tail-points** resemble rose-prickles. The appressed **toes** seem a single slender spine, but are often thrown apart. Two red **eyes** are distinct. It is not rare in the Tay tide-pools.

Length, $_1\frac{1}{65}$ inch. **Habitat.** Tay tide-pools. P.H.G.]

COLURUS GRALLATOR, *Gosse* (169), (Pl. XXXI. fig. 43).

[SP. CII. **Lorica** *much compressed; lateral outline ovate, sub-square behind, without points;* **toes** *half as long as lorica, very slender, straight, readily separated; ventral cleft slightly narrowed in the middle.*

Nearly related to the preceding; but the outline, viewed dorsally, is longer and narrower; there is no protrusion of the body behind the lorica; and the **toes** are quite straight. The frontal **hook** is unusually narrow. I have not been sure of an eye. A dozen examples have occurred from the Tay tide-pools.

Length, $_7\frac{1}{50}$ inch. **Habitat.** Tay tide-pools. P.H.G.]

COLURUS MICROMELA, *Gosse* (Pl. XXXI. fig. 45).

Monura micromela . . . . . Gosse (169).

[SP. CII. **Lorica** *in dorsal aspect broadly ovate, produced behind into slightly projecting points, separated by a shallow rounded sinus; in lateral aspect the quadrant of an oval;* **foot** *small;* **toes** *of uniform excessive tenuity.*

I have had, for thirty-six years, drawings of a species which I had marked (with " ? ") as *Monura dulcis*. Very recently, in water from Slough, what seems the same form, now figured, has occurred, and that repeatedly. The excessive tenuity of the toes¹ is the most striking feature; and then the round sinus between the lorica-points. No eye is visible. The general figure is that of *Col. bicuspidatus*.

Length, $_7\frac{1}{50}$ inch. **Habitat.** Lacustrine. P.H.G.]

---

¹ In page 367 of the *Journ. Roy. Micr. Soc.*, 1887, Mr. Gosse says "I have seen the toes widely expanded. The species must therefore be transferred to *Colurus*."

COLURUS LEPTUS, *Gosse* (170), (Pl. XXXI. fig. 46).

[SP. CII. **Lorica**, *in dorsal aspect, long oval; in lateral aspect, abruptly excavate behind; dorsal hind points, acute; ventral cleft close, insensibly expanding to a long pyriform foot-orifice;* **toe** *a slender style, apparently undivided;* **foot** *and toe about half as long as lorica; one large* **eye** *in occiput.*

A marked character, very easily recognisable, is the hind excavation of the lorica, as if a slice had been cut clean out. Examples with this peculiarity are quite common, both from weedy fresh waters, and from rock-pools on our northern and southern coasts. And I can trace no difference between them, save that the marine examples may be a trifle stouter in outline. The toe is a slender produced point, I will not say indivisible, but not, in my experience, divided. Several oil-globules are usually present in the dorsal part of the visceral cavity.

Length. Extended, $\frac{1}{300}$ inch. **Habitat.** Lacustrine and marine. P.H.G.]

METOPIDIA PYGMÆA, *Gosse* (171), (Pl. XXXI. fig. 47).

[SP. CII. **Lorica** *ovate, much elevated, the back rounded, the edges overhanging; hind margin rounded; ventral surface flat;* **foot** *stout, long;* **toe** *apparently single, small, acute.*

This seems the smallest of the genus; smaller than *emarginata*, or than *triptera*, which latter was in sight at the same time, for comparison. It is very transparent and colourless, the viscera only just discernible; the **trophi**, though working, were but shadowy lines. The extremity of the lorica is neither pointed, nor sinuate, but evenly round : its overhanging margins are remarkable, recalling *Notholca scapha.* There are two clear colourless globules at the very front, remote from each other, probably eyes. The frontal hook is carried rather close to the front, and seems incapable of independent motion ; it is visible in a dorsal view, as a line parallel to the front. Two minute air-bubbles were in the alimentary canal of the individual examined ; but no particles, nor stain, of food, though the tiny creature was industriously picking all the time it was under observation—an hour or more. It was active and restless, creeping about the floccose, but rarely swimming, and then laboriously. A single specimen occurred in a phial of *Utricularia* sent by Mr. W. R. Hood, from the middle of Ireland.

Length. Extended, $\frac{1}{350}$ inch. P.H.G.]

METOPIDIA OVALIS, *Ehrenberg*, (Pl. XXXIV. fig. 2).

Lepadella ovalis[1] . . . . Ehrenberg (42).

SP. CII. **Lorica** *depressed, oval, narrowed in front ; dorsal plate truncated at both ends, its margin not excised.*

Ehrenberg draws the ventral plate with a deep, square excision in front, and a small arched one behind. He notices that the unci are one-toothed ; the **gastric glands** circular ; the œsophagus short, and the **eyes** absent.

Length, $\frac{1}{310}$ inch. **Habitat.** Paris, Copenhagen, Berlin (Ehr.).

METOPIDIA EMARGINATA, *Ehrenberg* (Pl. XXXIV. fig. 6).

Lepadella emarginata . . . Ehrenberg (42).

SP. CII. **Lorica** *depressed, oval, broad in front; dorsal plate excised at both ends.* **Length** (without the foot), $\frac{1}{15}$ inch. **Habitat.** Berlin (Ehr.).

METOPIDIA (?) SALPINA *Ehrenberg* (Pl. XXXIV. fig. 4).

Lepadella (?) salpina . . . Ehrenberg (42).

SP. CII. **Lorica** *oblong, prismatic, obtusely triangular with a dorsal crest.* This should possibly be referred to Mr. Gosse's genus *Diplax.* The lorica is ren-

---

[1] The reasons for uniting the genera *Lepadella, Squamella,* and *Metopidia* have been given in vol. ii. p. 106.

dered uneven by fine depressions; and the posterior end of the crest projects somewhat beyond the base of the foot.

Length (of lorica), $_{5}\frac{1}{6}$ inch. **Habitat.** Berlin (Ehr.).

METOPIDIA CORNUTA, *Schmarda* (Pl. XXXIV. fig. 8).

Lepadella cornuta . . . . . . Schmarda (135).

SP. CH. **Lorica** *oval ; its anterior margin with two great spines.*

Body yellowish grey. A deep gap separates the two curved frontal horns. The **unci** are one-toothed. Schmarda says that there are two **contractile vesicles** at the foot ; and he draws two small vesicles in that position. Unfortunately he does not say whether he has seen them contract or not; nor whether they did so independently of each other. The only similar case of such a construction, that I am acquainted with, is that of *Conochilus volvox* (according to Cohn, vol. i. p. 90, foot note).

Length (total), $_{100}\frac{1}{0}$ inch. **Habitat.** Brackish water, New Orleans (Schm.).

METOPIDIA OBLONGA, *Ehrenberg* (Pl. XXXIV. 5).

Squamella oblonga . . . . . Ehrenberg (42).

SP. CH. **Lorica** *elliptical, or ovately oblong, hyaline ; toes long, slender ; eyes four.*

There are two or three teeth in each **uncus**; the **gastric glands** are pear-shaped; and there are four frontal **eyes** arranged in the angles of a parallelogram. Ehrenberg has seen a **contractile vesicle**, and lateral canals.

Length (total), $_{7}\frac{1}{6}$ inch. **Habitat.** Berlin (Ehr.).

HEXASTEMMA MELANOGLENA, LEPADELLA MUCRONATA, L. SETIFERA, SQUAMELLA QUADRIDENTATA, *Schmarda* (135). These possibly may be *Metopidiæ*, but see note 1, Sup^{t}, p. 8.

MONURA DULCIS, *Ehrenberg* (12), (Pl. XXXIV. fig. 9).

SP. CH. **Lorica** *ovate, obliquely truncate behind, acute ; eyes distant.*

The dorsal outline (a long narrow oval, truncate at both ends), the pointed termination of the lorica (seen at the side view), and the wide separation of the eyes, sufficiently distinguish this species; which, Ehrenberg thought, might be marine as well as lacustrine.

Length, $_{2}\frac{1}{8}\frac{1}{8}$ inch. **Habitat.** Near Berlin ; possibly Cattaro (Ehr.).

Genus DISPINTHERA, *Gosse* (171).

GEN. CH. **Body** *sub-cylindric, inclosed, in part, within a* **lorica** *open in front and in rear, apparently cleft down the venter ; head and foot habitually protruded ;* **head** *distinct, protected by horny plates, but without a frontal* **hook** *; two cervical* **eyes.**

DISPINTHERA CAPSA, *Gosse* (171), (Pl. XXXI. fig. 48).

[SP. CH. **Lorica** *in most parts soft and flexible ; foot stout ; toes two, furcate, thick, straight, tapering, acute.*

This apparently new form I found in the sediment of water dipped by Mr. Dolton from "ditch No. 2," in Sutton Park, Birmingham, crowded with fine Desmidieæ. The facies strikes one as very peculiar, and difficult to explain. The **front** is capable of much protrusion, in a conical form, where a globose tubercle is visible, but only occasionally, and a similar one, but more constant, on the occiput (or rather crown of the head), just below the point of the occipital sheath. The lorica is discernible chiefly about the head ; it there projects into several points, which seem very flexible, but constant. When the head is far retracted (which is seldom), an array of spears is left bristling up. Now and then, at the pectus. the integument is seen to fall into a flap, or hanging lip, to be presently withdrawn. The principal shield protects the back of the head, but does not form an arching hood, or frontal hook. The trophi, in several good views, seemed of the pattern (fig. 89) of my Mem. "On Manduc. Org.," *Phil. Trans.* 1856) assigned to *Notomm. gibba.* The whole facies recalls one of the smaller *Notommatæ;* yet the two well-defined eyes remove it from them; besides the manifest lorica. It seems to approach the marine genus *Mytilia,* but not very close.

Only a single specimen occurred, in June. It was active and busy, constantly turning and wheeling about, but little given to locomotion. It suggests the odd notion of a creature carrying its great clumsy head in a bandbox.

Length, $\frac{1}{96}$ inch. **Habitat.** Lacustrine. P.H.G.]

MONURA BARTONIA, *Gosse* (171), (Pl. XXXI. fig. 49).

[SP. CH. **Lorica** *ovate, moderately compressed, dorsal outline (viewed laterally) one-third of a circle, ending in triangular points, which have the dorsal side slightly excavate; one* **eye** *frontal;* **toe** *straight, slender, acute, more than half as long as the lorica, shouldered dorsally.*

The genera *Colurus* and *Monura* (if, indeed, they are not one) appear to contain a large number of species, peculiarly difficult to define satisfactorily. Yet this and the following are, I think, to be distinguished. The toe and **foot** together are nearly equal in length to the lorica. I could find no trace of a median line in the toe. Its extreme length and tenuity are notable. Each posterior point of the lorica forms an equilateral triangle, clearly defined from the general area of the lorica, by a line—the base of the triangle. These two triangular termini are of excessive delicacy, and may easily escape a cursory notice. On the extreme front, under the frontal hook, is a small dark crimson **eye,** like a wart on the face.

Its manners are those of so many of its fellows, remaining long totally withdrawn between the closed lorica-plates in front, pivoting and swaying on the toe-tip incessantly for hours. I first obtained it, in the spring of this year, from a pond known as the Reservoir, at Barton, near Torquay. Since then I have met with single specimens from many localities, and in abundance in the Kingskerswell mill-stream.

Length (from hook to toe-tip), $\frac{1}{113}$ inch. **Habitat.** Barton; Kingskerwell. P.H.G.]

MONURA LONCHERES, *Gosse* (171), (Pl. XXXI. fig. 50).

[SP. CH. **Dorsal outline** *narrowly ovate,* **lateral** *nearly semicircular;* **lorica** *rounded behind, with a median angular notch;* **toe** *shouldered dorsally, excessively long and slender.*

The most striking points in this beautiful species are its great depth (from back to belly), making about a half-circle, and the tenuity of the **toe,** which seems indivisible. This runs to so exceedingly fine a point as to escape notice, except with the most delicate focusing; even with a quarter objective, and the best possible light. The foot, of two condyliform joints, and the toe, together, are fully equal to the lorica in length; viz. $\frac{1}{115}$ inch. The ventral cleft is narrow, straight-sided, slightly approximate in front, and reaching round to the occiput, posteriorly to a short acute sinus whose sides form a right angle. There is a brilliant ruby **eye** about the middle of a saccate brain, and therefore cervical.

I have examined a number of examples, at different times, in sea-water obtained by Mr. Hood from the Invergowrie tide-pools. In one of these I timed the period of emptying the **contractile vesicle** to be just three minutes. It had this peculiarity, that the emptying was but partial on each occasion; that the bladder suddenly diminished its volume, but not to a point, *nor nearly.* The animal's posturing manners are exactly the same as described in the preceding species.

Length (total), $\frac{1}{105}$ inch. **Habitat.** Invergowrie tide-pools. P.H.G.]

MYTILIA PŒCILOPS, *Gosse* (171), (Pl. XXXI. fig. 51).

[SP. CII. **Lorica** *pergamentaceous, very flexible, constantly thrown into irregular folds, whence the outline is very variable ; the face, in particular, is capable of great protrusion in wide plicate membranes ; prevalent figure, foot, and toes, much as in M. teresa.*

Though this has many features in common with *tavina* and *teresa*, particularly the foot and toes, it has important peculiarities. The *dorsal* outline is like that of the latter, the lateral that of the former ; but *both* more rough and uncouth. The skin thrown irregularly into coarse rude folds, occurring at intervals at every part, precludes any fixed form, so that the figure accurately copied has become in a few minutes, though gradually, flagrantly incorrect. The **front** is large and broadly truncate, capable of pushing out, from its lower part, great membranous sacs and folds, which slowly change every moment, and the use of which is inexplicable. These expansions do not appear to be ciliated. The **mastax** and **trophi** are as in its congeners ; there is an ample brain, which carries a cervical red **eye**. The whole back is ridged—tectiform, not keeled.

I have observed numerous examples in sea-water from the Invergowrie tide-pools. They have all been remarkably heavy and sluggish in manners, little given to locomotion, wholly lacking the sprightly vivacity of the kindred species, and unusually intolerant of captivity. The abdominal viscera are generally of a rich orange-brown hue, and the whole tissues are more or less suffused with the same colour.

Length (lorica), $_2\frac{1}{4}_0$ inch. **Habitat.** Invergowrie, tide-pools. P.H.G.]

MYTILIA PRODUCTA, *Gosse* (171), (Pl. XXXI. fig. 53).

[SP. CII. **Skin** *flexible, plicate ;* **body** *slender, very extensile ;* **eye** *single, frontal ;* **foot** *and toes nearly as in* M. teresa.

The **lorica**, flexible in *M. pœcilops*, is perhaps even more so in this species, and recognisable only at the posterior extremity, where each lateral plate can be traced, as, with a rounded end, it curves under the trunk, to approach its fellow-plate, leaving a narrow ventral cleft. The **face** is quite truncate, slightly oblique, not abnormally developed. When gliding rapidly along a seaweed, the animal is very worm-like, the body and the foot, about equal in length, forming two successive cylinders, the latter half as thick as the former. But both, especially the **foot**, are capable of sudden elongation at will. Thus the creature has a facies which distinguishes it from either of its congeners. Perhaps it comes nearest to *teresa*. The **toes** are even broader proportionally ; together much exceeding the width of the foot whence they issue. The **eye** is conspicuous, nearly frontal, but changes its position with the brain. The whole animal is colourless, but very full of folds and corrugations. Very long **mucous glands** proceed from the toes through the whole of the foot.

The species first occurred to my observation on May 7, 1887, on very fine seaweeds (*Ceramium*), which I gathered in the deep cup-like pool in limestone rock at Oddicombe Point. I met with about half-a-dozen examples.

Length, $_1\frac{1}{6}_5$ inch. **Habitat.** Marine, Devonshire. P.H.G.]

MYTILIA TERESA, *Gosse* (169), (Pl. XXXI. fig. 52).

[SP. CII. **Body** *truly oval ;* **toes** *together wider than foot ; each toe large, long, ovate, abruptly produced to a long, slender, acute point.*

This very pleasing species I have found in some abundance, in water dipped for me out of tide-pools in various parts of Torbay by my little granddaughter, with whose name I honour it. It has a very distinct red **eye** in the occiput. The large bulbous toes are peculiar. It is a sprightly creature, playing actively among confervoid algæ, often pivoting on its toes, like a *Cathypna*, jerking and bowing ; it is less locomotive than *M. Tavina*.

Length, $_2\frac{1}{6}_0$ inch. **Habitat.** Marine, Torbay. P.H.G.]

J.

PTERODINA REFLEXA, *Gosse* (169), (Pl. XXXI. fig. 54).

[SP. CH. **Lorica** *elliptical in outline, the two longitudinal halves bent upward and backward, at a considerable angle ; the dorsal surface being evenly furrowed, the ventral rounded.*

The angular character is not noticed on a dorsal view, but becomes conspicuous in the act of turning. *P. valvata* bends its leaves *downward*, on hinges, at will. *P. reflexa* bends its halves *upward*, on a medial line which is not hinged, but permanent. It is somewhat like a butterfly, sitting, with half-opened wings, on a flower in an autumn noon. The internal structure is normal.

Length (of lorica), $\frac{1}{210}$ inch. **Habitat.** Smallheath, Birmingham. P.H.G.]

BRACHIONUS BREVISPINUS, *Ehrenberg* (42), (Pl. XXXIV. fig. 17).

SP. CH. **Lorica** *smooth, with six sharp unequal* **occipital spines**, *and four stout* **posterior spines**, *of which the middle pair is the shorter.*

This Rotiferon closely resembles *B. Bakeri*, from which it differs mainly in the smoothness of its **lorica**, the length and shape of the **spines** (all very variable characteristics), and the form of its **gastric glands** ; each of the latter of which consists of two oval lobes.

Length, $\frac{1}{60}$ inch. **Habitat.** Near Berlin (Ehr.).

BRACHIONUS POLYCERUS, *Schmarda* (135), (Pl. XXXIV. fig. 13).

SP. CH. **Lorica** *broad, nearly six-sided; eight* **occipital spines**, *the outmost pair rough ; four* **posterior spines**, *the outer pair very long, the inner pair short.*

The **lorica** is flat and yellowish, and its pair of **occipital spines**, which are next to the outmost, cross these latter very curiously. Both the pairs of **posterior spines** curve inwards ; the middle pair very much so.

Length (of lorica), cir. $\frac{1}{100}$ inch. **Habitat.** Kingston, Jamaica (Schmarda).

BRACHIONUS ANCYLOGNATHUS, *Schmarda* (135), (Pl. XXXIV. fig. 14).

SP. CH. **Lorica** *broad, narrowed in front;* **occipital spines** *six ; the* **pectoral margin** *undulated, with two* **lateral spines** *; four* **posterior spines**, *the two outer the longer.*

Schmarda describes the shape of the **lorica** (which will be best understood from the figure), and adds that the **corona** is reddish, and three-lobed; the **eye** transversely oval.

Length, $\frac{1}{100}$ inch. **Habitat.** Stagnant water near Quito (Schmarda).

BRACHIONUS INERMIS, *Schmarda* (134), (Pl. XXXIV. fig. 18).

SP. CH. **Lorica** *smooth, anterior margin slightly concave ; no* **spines** *either in front or behind.*

From a slight sketch of a solitary specimen found in Egypt.

Length, $\frac{1}{100}$ inch. **Habitat.** Nile overflow, Monfalut (Schmarda).

BRACHIONUS LATISSIMUS, *Schmarda* (134), (Pl. XXXIV. fig. 15).

SP. CH. **Lorica** *very broad, rough ; six unequal* **occipital spines**, *none behind.*

The figure of this Egyptian *Brachionus*, as given by Schmarda, is very striking. The **lorica**, which is rough and of unusual breadth, is widest behind, and gradually narrows to the anterior margin, so that it has a trapezoidal shape. The posterior corners are rounded off, and the foot-opening is a shallow concavity. The anterior margin is scolloped so as to have six short pointed spines, with broad bases ; the middle and outmost pairs being rather the longest.

Length, $\frac{1}{10}$ inch. **Habitat.** Irrigation water in Egypt (Schmarda).

BRACHIONUS PUSTULATUS, *Schmarda* (135), (Pl. XXXIV. fig. 16).

SP. CII. **Lorica** *broad, covered with papillæ, the middle part of the dorsal surface raised in the shape of a rhombus ;* occipital spines *six ;* the posterior spines *four, equal.*

The **pectoral margin** is nearly straight, with a slight notch in the middle ; no **toes** observed on the foot. [Probably retracted. C.T.H.]

Length (of lorica), $\frac{1}{100}$ inch. **Habitat.** St. Juan del Norte, Central America (Schmarda).

BRACHIONUS LONGIPES, *Schmarda* (135), (Pl. XXXIV. fig. 20).

SP. CII. **Lorica** *trapezoidal ;* occipital spines *six ;* pectoral margin *without spines ;* foot *double the length of the body.*

Of the six **occipital spines** the middle are the longest, and are curved outwards ; the outer somewhat shorter and turned inwards ; and the intermediate the shortest, and almost perpendicular. The **pectoral margin** is slightly curved, and has a small notch. The foot-opening, in the lorica, is semicircular, and without processes. The **toes** are short.

Total length, $\frac{1}{10}$ inch. **Habitat.** Near Pasto, New Granada (Schm.).

BRACHIONUS LEYDIGII, *Cohn* (21), (Pl. XXXIV. fig. 19).

SP. CII. **Lorica** *sub-quadrate with six nearly equal* occipital spines ; *the* pectoral margin *arched, with a sharp notch in the middle ; the hind end triangular, obtusely excised ; the dorsal surface marked with polygonal tessellations, which are themselves covered with a fine network of markings ; the* foot *transversely contractile ; the* ephippial egg *rough with papillæ.*

The most noticeable points about this *Brachionus* are its tessellate dorsal plate, and its foot. The former has twenty-one tessellations, arranged in five vertical rows (two lateral of four each, two next of five each, and a central row of three), while the latter, according to Cohn, admits of being greatly compressed *transversely*, so as to look like a thin band. The **lateral canals** also have unusually large loops and coils. The **contractile vesicle** is large, and so are the egg-shaped **gastric glands.**

Length (total), cir. $\frac{1}{70}$ inch.

BRACHIONUS BUDAPESTINENSIS, *Daday* (208), (Pl. XXXIV. fig. 25).

SP. CII. **Lorica** *rough, tessellated dorsally and ventrally, rounded and spineless behind ;* occipital spines *four, the middle pair curved downwards and outwards.*

This species is remarkable for the unusual shape of the tessellations of the **lorica**, especially on the dorsal side, where they are all bounded by curved lines. The minute papillæ of the lorica occur on all the spines. The **gastric glands** are pear-shaped with their pointed ends directed forwards ; and the inner surfaces of the **rami** are wavy, each showing six undulations.

Length. Not recorded. **Habitat.** Neighbourhood of Budapest (Daday).

BRACHIONUS QUADRATUS, *Rousselet* (Pl. XXXIV. figs. 11, 12).

SP. CII. **Lorica** *nearly square, rough with minute, irregular, polygonal areolations ;* dorsal plate *arched, sloping from behind forwards ;* occipital spines *six, the middle pair the longest ;* ventral plate *nearly flat, with an undulating mental edge ; three short spines, one mid-dorsal and two lateral, round the foot opening.*

This fine *Brachionus* was found by Mr. C. Rousselet, this year, in Epping Forest. The lorica when seen by $\frac{1}{4}$ inch obj. with dark field illumination, is as beautiful as it is singular; resembling very fine lace. Two low ridges run from its posterior dorsal edge, on either side of the median line, to the projecting spines; and, from the central strip contained between them, the lorica slopes rapidly to the edge of the ventral plate. There are faint traces of large tessellations along these two ridges. The foot is remarkable; for it has the false joints of a *Noteus* and, near the base, the usual transverse wrinkling of a *Brachionus*: the toes, too, are not only unusually long, but are themselves retractile like those of a *Philodina*.

Length (of lorica), $\frac{1}{7}$ by $\frac{1}{20}$ inch. **Habitat.** A pond in Epping Forest (Rousselet).

BRACHIONUS MILITARIS, *Ehrenberg* (42), (Pl. XXXIV. fig. 23).

Brachionus conium   .   Atwood (2).

SP. CII. **Lorica** *tessellated, both surfaces covered with raised points; ten* **spines** *in front, of which four are on the dorsal margin, four on the ventral, and two where the margins meet; also four spines behind, the middle pair (between which the foot issues) being of marked unequal length.*

Ehrenberg says that *militaris* has a rough lorica, and no fewer than twelve **spines** in front; but Cohn (*loc. cit.*) describes it as tessellated, and as having only ten spines in front.[1] Curiously enough, of the two figures in which Ehrenberg appears to intend to show all the spines, one has only ten spines in front, and the other eleven. Cohn's figures make the lorica distinctly unsymmetrical throughout, a feature almost lost in those of Ehrenberg. The two middle front dorsal spines are longer than any of the other anterior ones; they are generally curved downwards, and are not unfrequently twisted awry; Mr. Atwood's figure (*loc. cit.*) shows them bent, half way up, at right angles to their usual direction. The posterior, unequal pair, which guard the exit of the foot, have the right hand spine (dorsal view) much the longer of the two; and the outer posterior pair, at the angles of the lorica, are also of unequal length.

This Rotiferon has a very large **contractile vesicle**; which, according to Cohn, occupies, when fully expanded, two-thirds of the body-cavity. He also describes it as consisting of two chambers,[2] and states that, on mixing a little indigo in the water, he has seen fine particles of the pigment drawn up through the cloaca into the contractile vesicle, and again expelled from it over the same path.

Mr. D. Bryce, who found this *Brachionus* lately near London, says, " the foot-orifice seems to be twisted on one side, so that the spines bounding it are in different planes; the left-hand and smaller spine being altogether depressed below the right-hand one, and pointing slightly downwards. The solitary dorsal **antenna** is moderately stout, and furnished with very distinct long setæ; but I could not make out the paired lateral antennæ. The **eye** is large, and situated at the hinder end of a large **brain**. The **gastric glands** are triangular. The animal is fond of rotating, in one spot, round its longer axis, just like *Synchæta tremula*, though I could see no trace of an anchoring ' cable.' "

Length (of lorica), from $\frac{1}{155}$ to $\frac{1}{130}$ inch (D. Bryce). **Habitat.** Berlin (Ehrenberg); near London (D. Bryce); Queensland (V. G. Thorpe); Philadelphia, U.S. (Leidy).

BRACHIONUS POLYACANTHUS, *Ehrenberg* (42), (Pl. XXXIV. fig. 24).

SP. CII. **Lorica** *smooth; with four long* **occipital spines**; *the* **pectoral margin** *six-toothed; posterior spines* *five, the two outer of which are very long.*

---

[1] Mr. V. Gunson Thorpe, Surgeon, R.N., and Mr. D. Bryce have obliged me with characteristic drawings, which they have made, of specimens found by the former at Brisbane, and by the latter near London. Each of these observers figures the tessellations, the ten anterior spines, and the general lack of symmetry of the lorica. Professor Leidy also has favoured me with an excellent drawing of the dorsal surface from an American specimen.

[2] The contractile vesicles of *Asplanchna Ebbesbornii*, of *Scaridium eudactylotum*, and of other Rotifera, have also this chambered appearance; which is due to the construction of the surface by very fine muscular threads.

The **pectoral margin**, in Ehrenberg's drawing, cannot strictly be said to show spines; but it is notched so as to have six very small projections. The **four occipital spines** are of nearly equal length; and the very long **posterior spines** spring from the outer corners of the dorsal surface. Three short spines surround the opening for the foot. Cohn thinks that Ehrenberg has made a mistake in giving this *Brachionus* three spines round the foot-opening, and has himself described (21), as *polyacanthus*, a *Brachionus* which has only two spines at the foot-opening.

It is clear, however, from his description and drawing, that Cohn's animal is the variety of *B. pala* given in Pl. XXVIII. fig. 3. Ehrenberg says that the **unci** are four-toothed, and the **gastric glands** nearly circular. He makes no remark about the foot, but draws it jointed, like that of *B. militaris* or *Noteus quadricornis*.[1]

Length, ₁⅟₁₀ inch. **Habitat.** Berlin (Ehr.).

B. COSTULATUS, *Eichwald* (167), (Pl. XXXIV. fig. 21). SP. CH. Lorica *with six short nearly equal* **occipital spines,** *and diminishing to a rounded, spineless end, behind; longitudinal ridges run from the tip of each spine to the points of a zig-zag transverse ridge just below the level of the eye ;* **foot** *with four to six toes.* I give this description from Eichwald's, but it is difficult to believe in a *Brachionus* with half-a-dozen toes. The transverse ridge is the boundary of a series of tessellations which cover the lorica, but which are not given in the drawing, as they were rendered obscure by the viscera and contained food. Near St. Petersburg.

B. PLICATILIS, *Mobius* (117)=*B. Mülleri.* There are two remarkable statements in Herr Mobius' otherwise able memoir, which I think must be errors. In the first place, he considers the free end of the dorsal antenna to be the mouth. This needs no comment. In the second, he draws, and describes, no fewer than four other dorsal antennæ, viz. the two usual antennæ on the lumbar regions, and two more in the neck, on either side of the mastax. These latter are due, I think, to some error of observation. Certainly there was nothing of the kind in the specimens of *Mülleri* that I obtained from brackish ditches in Bedminster, near Clifton.

B. CHILENSIS, *Schmarda* (135)=slight var. of *B. Bakeri.*

B. TESTUDO, *Ehrenberg* (48); B. BIDENS, *Plate* (126); B. MINIMUS, *Bartsch* (8).

All these appear to be examples of *B. angularis.*

B. JAMAICENSIS ; B. NICARAGUENSIS ; B. SYENENSIS ; *Schmarda* (135, 134). All these three species of Schmarda's seem but varieties of *urceolaris.*

B. DIACANTHUS, *Schmarda* (135) ; B. DECIPIENS, *Plate* (126) ; B. MARGOI, *Daday* (32).

All these appear to be varieties of the very variable form *B. pala* ; see vol. ii. p. 117.

B. LOTHARINGIUS, *Imhof* (179)=*B. dorcas.*

B. HEPATOTOMUS, *Gosse* (54)=*B. Mülleri.*

B. GLEASONII=*Anuræa Gleasonii*, Up de Graf (149), (Pl. XXXIV. fig. 22). SP. CH. Dorsal plate *of lorica rough, arched, oblong-square in outline, with the two posterior corners cut off, and four curved* spines *projecting from the four angles thus formed :* anterior margin, *of each plate, spineless, but with a median projecting cusp ; a curved* spine *on the mid-dorsal line ;* ventral plate *smooth, flat.*

This curious creature was discovered at Elmira in 1883 by Dr. Up de Graf, who states that the ventral plate ends in a long tapering straight spine. Mr. C. M. Vorce, however, to whom I am indebted for a drawing, says that this so-called spine is only a jointed foot, like that of *Noteus.*

---

[1] I had thought of removing *B. militaris* and *B. polyacanthus* from the genus *Brachionus*, on account of their jointed, unwrinkled foot, like that of a *Noteus.* But after I had seen Mr. Rousselet's *B. quadratus*, with its jointed foot, wrinkled at the base, I thought it better to make no change; especially as I have never seen *B. militaris* or *B. polyacanthus.*

Genus SCHIZOCERCA, *Daday* (207).

GEN. CH. *A genus of the* Brachionidæ, *with a long* **foot** *ending in a fork of two unequal branches, each terminated by a pair of unequal toes.*

SCHIZOCERCA DIVERSICORNIS, *Daday* (207), (Pl. XXXIV. fig. 10).

SP. CII. **Body** *long, wider in front, tapering behind;* **lorica** *smooth, with four* **anterior spines,** *the middle pair small, broad-based, the marginal pair long, sharp, curved;* **ventral margin** *excised in the middle; two unequal* **posterior spines,** *the right much the longer, sharper, and incurved; the left shorter and broader.*

The **lorica** is a long oval; it really has only two anterior spines, one on either side, at the junctions of the occipital and mental edges. The two so-called middle spines are formed by the edges of the usual dorsal notch (for the dorsal antenna), and by those of the shallow circular excavations in the lorica, on either side of the notch. The posterior spines are even more unequal than those of *B. militaris*; and the forked foot with its two pairs of unequal toes reminds one of those of *Philodina macrostyla* (Pl. XXXII. fig. 6 b).

Length, ₁⁴₅ to ₁²₇ inch. **Habitat.** Neighbourhood of Budapest (Daday).

ANURÆA QUADRIDENTATA, *Ehrenberg* (42), (Pl. XXXIV. fig. 29).

SP. CII. **Lorica** *oblong, tessellated; with four* **occipital spines;** *rounded and spineless behind.*

Length (of lorica without the spines), ₂|₆ inch. **Habitat.** Berlin (Ehr.).

ANURÆA SQUAMULA, *Ehrenberg* (42), (Pl. XXXIV. fig. 28).

SP. CII. **Lorica** *obtusely quadrate, smooth, with six* **anterior spines;** *rounded and spineless behind.*

The only peculiarity noticed by Ehrenberg is its "very large, sparkling, round, red, **eye.**"

Length, ₂|₆ to ₄|₅ inch. **Habitat.** Copenhagen, Ingoldstadt, Berlin (Ehr.).

ANURÆA FALCULATA, *Ehrenberg* (42), (Pl. XXXIV. fig. 26).

SP. CII. **Lorica** *oblong, rough; with six* **anterior spines,** *the middle pair sickle-shaped; rounded and spineless behind.*

Ehrenberg says the **gastric glands** are large.

Length, ₁|₁ inch. **Habitat.** Berlin (Ehr.).

ANURÆA BIREMIS, *Ehrenberg* (42), (Pl. XXXIV. fig. 32).

SP. CH. **Lorica** *linear, elongated, with four* **occipital spines;** *dorsal surface very smooth, with two sharp, moveable, oar-shaped processes, one on each side.*

There are three teeth in each **uncus,** round **gastric glands,** and a red, round, sparkling **eye.** The **side spines** are weak and pliable.

Length, ₁|₁ inch. **Habitat.** Sea-water, near Kiel (Ehr.).

ANURÆA STIPITATA, *Ehrenberg* (42), (Pl. XXXIV. fig. 27).

SP. CII. **Lorica** *subquadrate or triangular, ending behind in a simple spine; six* **spines** *in front;* **dorsal plate** *tessellated.*

The points of difference between this species and *cochlearis* are given in vol ii. p. 124. Ehrenberg notices that *stipitata* has a great red cervical **eye,** and further says that he once saw something like an **antenna** (Respirationsröhre) on the *ventral* side, when looking at the animal sidewise. His figure shows the creature with its head drawn into its lorica, and a very broad, stout, clove-shaped antenna hanging over the middle of the mental edge of the lorica. It is, of course, just possible that the dorsal antenna might take such a position, if the head were much curved to the ventral surface : but I have never seen anything like it.

Length, $\frac{1}{180}$ to $\frac{1}{240}$ inch. Habitat. Berlin (Ehr.).

ANURÆA TESTUDO, *Ehrenberg* (42), (Pl. XXXIV. fig. 31).

SP. CH. **Lorica** *quadrate ; with six straight and nearly equal* **spines** *in front, and two short spines behind ; both* **dorsal** *and* **ventral plates** *rough, the former tessellated.*

This species differs from *aculeata* in the near equality in length of the front **spines,** the shortness of the hind ones, and the roughness of the ventral surface, all characters of somewhat doubtful constancy. Ehrenberg says that there are four teeth in each **uncus,** that the **gastric glands** (unlike those of *serrulata*) have no stalks to attach them to the stomach, and that the **eye** is transversely oval. He also says that besides a smooth-surfaced **egg** he has seen a faceted one ; which latter he supposes to be ephippial.

Length, $\frac{1}{210}$ to $\frac{1}{240}$ inch. Habitat. Berlin (Ehr.).

ANURÆA VALGA, *Ehrenberg* (42), (Pl. XXXIV. fig. 30).

SP. CH. **Lorica** *quadrate ; with six* **spines** *in front, of which the two mid-spines are the longest, and two unequal spines behind ;* **dorsal** *and anterior portion of* **ventral plate** *rough, the former also tessellated.*

Another species resembling *aculeata.* Ehrenberg says, however, that the teeth in its **uncus** are five in number, while those in *aculeata* are many. The **gastric glands** are egg-shaped ; and the red **eye,** transversely oval.

Length, $\frac{1}{240}$ inch. Habitat. Berlin (Ehr.).

ANURÆA SCHISTA, *Gosse* (171), (Pl. XXXI. fig. 55).

[SP. CH. **Lorica** *oblong, tapering to a short spine behind ;* **dorsal plate** *tessellated in polygonal areas on each side of a mesial ridge, and punctured ;* **ventral plate** *much shorter, produced into a projecting sharp point, divided from the dorsal by a deep cleft.*

It has relations with *stipitata* and *cochlearis* ; in tessellation agreeing with the latter, and with *tecta.* The anterior **spines** are straight. It is evidently an approach to *Notholca,* but I do not see the ridges and furrows descending from the spines. The **tessellæ** are somewhat coarse and ill-defined. The straight short antlers, and the great descending point of the ventral plate, distinguish it at once from every known species. This point is a stiff taper spine : sometimes it projects obliquely (*b*) ; then, in a moment it is jerked in, so as to be quite hidden, only to be as rapidly thrown out again. Even in a dorsal view it can be clearly seen, through the transparent tissues. I believe I have seen, on two occasions, a discharged egg, carried under the belly, in the manner of *tecta,* &c. The **eye** is a ball of deep red, of enormous size. A very large **contractile vesicle,** when full, forces up the other viscera to the middle of the body : when, often, the well-defined contrast between the dark turbid contents of the intestine, and the crystal clearness of the bladder, is curious and striking. The bladder has no effect on the ventral spine, whose movements are manifestly voluntary. It is a sprightly active swimmer.

Length, $\frac{1}{102}$ inch. Habitat. Birmingham. P.H.G.]

A. LONGISTYLA, *Schmarda* (135) = *A. cochlearis* (vol. ii. p. 124).

A. REGALIS, *Imhof* (179) = var. of *A. aculeata* (vol. ii. p. 123).

A. INERMIS, *Ehrenberg* (42) ; like *Notholca acuminata,* but without frontal spines ; and with a feeble bent lorica, and indistinct longitudinal striæ : Ehrenberg only saw one specimen, and it is difficult to say what it was.

NOTHOLCA FOLIACEA, *Ehrenberg* (Pl. XXXIV. fig. 35).

Anuræa foliacea . . . . . . Ehrenberg (42).

SP. CH. **Lorica** *oblong, with six* **spines** *in front, and tapering to one spine behind ;* **dorsal and ventral surfaces** *with longitudinal ridges and a rough zone in front.*

This *Anuræa* of Ehrenberg's will fall into Mr. Gosse's new genus of *Notholca.* Ehrenberg gives few details of its structure, but notices that there are four teeth in each uncus, and that there is an obvious brain lying under the eye.

Length, $\frac{1}{100}$ inch. **Habitat.** Berlin (Ehr.).

NOTHOLCA HEPTODON, *Perty* (Pl. XXXIV. fig. 34).

Anuræa heptodon . . . . Perty (124).

SP. CH. **Lorica** *an elongated oblong, with a wavy striated surface ; with six* **spines** *in front, and tapering to a short, sharp, slightly upturned spine behind ;* **dorsal plate** *convex ;* **ventral** *concave, and so set that its side view of the lorica is not wedge-shaped but box-like.*

This *Notholca* was discovered by Perty at Bern, and described from a solitary specimen. Mr. T. Smithson Spencer has lately found what, I think, is the same creature, at Rochdale, and has favoured me with a drawing of it. Both observers describe the **lorica** as unfaceted and with wavy longitudinal ridges and outline.

Mr. Spencer says that a membrane connects the two plates behind ; and that he has seen them drawn together, with the membrane projecting. in a fold, between them.

Length, $\frac{1}{44}$ inch. **Habitat.** Bern (Perty) ; Rochdale (T. S. Spencer).

NOTHOLCA STRIATA, *Ehrenberg* (Pl. XXXIV. fig. 33).

Anuræa striata . . . . Ehrenberg (12).
Anuræa baltica . . . . Eichwald (15).

SP. CH. **Lorica** *linear, elongated. with six* **spines** *in front, and rounded behind ; its* **dorsal plate** *with twelve longitudinal striæ.*

Müller discovered this *Notholca* in sea-water at Copenhagen in 1779, and gave three figures of it, of which one is probably a mistake for *Anuræa biremis* ; as it shows two curved spines on the under surface of the lorica. Ehrenberg found it both in fresh water and in the sea, and noticed that the membranaceous **lorica** changed its form with the contractions of the body. He also observed three teeth in each **uncus**, and a **nervous ganglion** close to the red **eye.** Eichwald's *Anuræa baltica* is probably the same animal. Eichwald's figure and description give only six longitudinal striæ ; the two mid-striæ stop short just above the mastax ; and the other four stop at the margin of a semicircular opening in the ventral plate. Probably the viscera obscured his view ; moreover he admits that occasionally he could see twelve longitudinal striæ.

Length, $\frac{1}{100}$ inch to $\frac{1}{44}$ inch. **Habitat.** Copenhagen (Müller) ; Berlin (Ehr.).

NOTHOLCA JUGOSA, *Gosse* (169), (Pl. XXXI. fig. 59).

[SP. CH. **Lorica** *ovato-rhomboid, highly elevated, broadly truncate before, narrowly behind ; ridges and furrows strongly marked, ending before they reach the hind margin.*

This, of all the *Notholcæ*, seems to come the nearest to Ehrenberg's figure of *Anuræa striata* ; of which he says, it is marine at Copenhagen, associating with *Pter. clypeata* and *Brach. Mülleri*, species with which *jugosa* is commonly found in the tide-pools of the Firth of Tay and of the Devon coast.

Length, $\frac{1}{190}$ inch to $\frac{1}{37}$ inch. **Habitat.** Marine. P.H.G.]

NOTHOLCA RHOMBOIDEA, *Gosse* (169), (Pl. XXXI. fig. 58).

[SP. CH. **Lorica** *rhomboidal, with lateral angles rounded, the front produced and truncate ;* **dorsal and ventral plates** *separated behind by a short cleft.*

The ridges, in this species, can with difficulty be discerned, especially as the rotating head is habitually protruded, which the creature does not retract for the shock of any tap or shake of the instrument that I can give. There is a long wrinkled œsophagus, a great saccate **stomach**, a distinct intestine, with the cloaca at the very extremity of the lorica : the **branchial bands** are distinct, but no contractile vesicle. It is not uncommon, with the preceding.

Length, $_1\frac{1}{6}_0$ inch to $_T\frac{1}{7}_T$ inch. **Habitat.** Marine. P.H.G.]

NOTHOLCA SPINIFERA, *Gosse* (169), (Pl. XXXI. fig. 57).

[SP. CH. **Lorica** broadly sub-rhomboidal ; the **dorsal plate** often less than the **ventral** and separated by a wide and deep cleft ; at each angle of junction is seated a short spine so hinged as to be concealed within the cleft, or widely projected, at will.

An interesting and attractive species. The whole interior is often richly coloured, especially the enormous **stomach**. An ample **contractile vesicle** is present. The hind outline in some examples is evenly rounded ; in others an inangulation marks both plates. Ehrenberg's figure of *Anur. biremis* may be compared with this ; but it differs in important details ; and his text gives no help. I received this also from the Tay tide-pools.

Length (of lorica), $_1\frac{1}{2}_0$ to $_1\frac{1}{6}_0$ inch. **Habitat.** Tay tide-pools. P.H.G.]

NOTHOLCA POLYGONA, *Gosse* (169), (Pl. XXXI. fig. 60).

[SP. CH. **Lorica** roundly pear-shaped, truncate in front ; the central pair of the **occipital spines** stout, the other two pairs almost obsolete ; **ventral plate** forming a square box, with sloping, many-angled sides.

A remarkable form. The **dorsal plate** is a half-oval, the ventral nearly flat. The latter is very peculiar : a kind of sub-cubic box, open at the summit, runs down to about three-fourths' length, and then proceeds, in pyramidal form, to a point at bottom ; and this appears to contain the viscera. Each side is covered in by a plate of two planes, but appears to be empty. On those parts of the arched dorsal plate which answer to these empty lateral chambers, run down very delicate flutings, while the broad medial part is quite clear and smooth. All the angles are distinct. The only example seen was dead, but showed a crimson **eye** and a normal **mastax.**

Length, $_1\frac{1}{6}_0$ inch. **Habitat.** Kingswood pool, near Birmingham. P.H.G.]

NOTHOLCA LABIS, *Gosse* (171), (Pl. XXXI. fig. 56).

[SP. CH. Almost the very counterpart of N. scapha, save that the outline is a longer oval, and the **lorica** is prolonged into a short, broad, truncate **tail** behind.

One of the discoveries of Mr. Hood of Dundee, who finds it numerous in a pool in Emmock Wood, near that city. He has repeatedly sent me specimens, but hitherto all have been dead on arrival. The little **tail** to the lorica reminds one of the handle of a dust-pan, if so homely an illustration can be tolerated. The ridges and furrows from the frontal spines are almost obliterate.

Length, $_3\frac{1}{1}_5$ inch. **Habitat.** Lacustrine, near Dundee (J.H.). P.H.G.]

Genus GOMPHOGASTER, *Force* (210).

GEN. CH. **Lorica** thick, box-like, enclosing the animal completely, except for a narrow slit-like opening upon the anterior ventral portion, cuneate in both dorsal and lateral aspects, triangular in transverse section, the ventral side the apical ; **foot** jointed, and usually retracted within the lorica ; **toe** apparently single ; **corona** apparently single, cilia robust, set in a single (?) marginal row, disc not much expanded beyond lorica when extended ; a stout retractile horn-like **process** protruded from each dorso-lateral corner of the lorica, when corona is extended.

GOMPHOGASTER AREOLATUS, *Vorce* (210), (Pl. XXXIV. fig. 36).

Plœsoma lenticulare . . . . . Herrick (175).

A single specimen was found by Mr. Vorce in 1882; it was taken living in filterings from the water of Lake Erie, at Cleveland, Ohio. **Lorica** thick and strong, dark coloured, marked all over with areolar depressions, very much resembling the markings of *Hemiaulus*; sides slightly concave, a deep plicate furrow across the back at the widest part, from which two deep sub-central furrows, and two shallow sub-marginal furrows, extend upon the dorsal surface to the posterior tip of the lorica; lateral margins of the dorsal front of lorica slightly produced, making the corners prominent. **Foot** stout, two-jointed; toe apparently single; retractile **horns** very slightly clavate. **Eye-spot** not observed, but if present would be usually concealed by the dark lorica. Cilia of the **corona** robust, in a single (?) marginal row. Animal very active and strong, pushing its way among masses of diatoms and flocculent matter, and when entangled freeing itself by vigorous kicks with its strong foot.[1] Mr. Herrick (who found this animal several times in a reservoir near Hebron, Ohio) says that there is a ventral prominence on the **head**, bearing several long setæ; that the **trophi** are feeble; the **eye** cervical, and seated on a considerable ganglion; and that the **foot** has two appressed toes.

Length, cir. $\frac{1}{160}$ inch.

DOUBTFUL AND REJECTED GENERA.

Genus ARTHROCANTHUS, *Schmarda* (184).

A genus formed to contain the varieties of *Brachionus pala* with long posterior processes on the lorica (vol. ii. p. 117; Pl. XXVIII. fig. 8).

Genus ASCOMORPHA, *Perty* (124).

The same as Mr. Gosse's genus *Sacculus*.

Genus BORTHRIOCERCA, *Eichwald* (167).

The only species, *affinis*, is evidently some Rotiferon belonging to the *Rattulidæ*, but the figure and description are too vague for its identification.

Genus CYCLOGLENA, *Ehrenberg* (42).

A genus formed by Ehrenberg to take *Notommatæ* with more eyes than three, in a cluster, in the neck. There are two species, *lupus* (Pl. XXXIII. 15) and *elegans*. The former has a cluster of red specks in the neck. It is like *N. aurita*, but has no auricles, and is said to vary in length from $\frac{1}{14}$ to $\frac{1}{4}$ inch—which seems incredible.

The latter, Ehrenberg himself marked as a doubtful species. It is $\frac{1}{200}$ inch in length, and the drawing (from which little can be learnt) shows a row of spots stretching from above the stomach for a quarter of the animal's length: these could scarcely be eyes. It was found in Nile water: *lupus*, at Berlin.

Genus CYSTOPHTHALMUS, *Corda* (23).

In this genus there is but one very doubtful Rotiferon, *C. Ehrenbergii* (Pl. XXXII. fig. 22). This creature reminds one of a *Taphrocampa*. It is grub-shaped, tapering at both ends, and divided into fourteen or fifteen segments by muscular rings. The last two segments are of very much smaller radius than the preceding one, and form a sort of tail. There are a few cilia, surrounding a buccal orifice, on the ventral surface. This opens into a short buccal funnel leading to a pear-shaped sac (fig. *b*), round the inner walls of which are arranged four pairs of jaws, like curved rami on a dumb-bell-shaped fulcrum. A shorter, ringed œsophagus connects this sac with a simple conical

---

[1] The whole of the above description, of this very curious Rotiferon, has been taken from Mr. C. M. Vorce's interesting paper (210), read before the American Society of Microscopists in 1887.

stomach. This latter bears no **gastric glands,** and ends in a very short intestine with a cloacal opening on the ventral surface, just before the tail. The **eye** is a refracting lens, resting on a top-shaped mass of purple-red pigment; and the whole is enclosed in an egg-shaped transparent capsule.

The only other organ is what appears to be a large, cylindrical, two-lobed **ovary,** lying on either side of the stomach. If the animal be a Rotiferon, it is very badly described. Herr Corda found it, in 1831, at the weirs between the islands of the Moldau, below Prague.

Length, $1\frac{1}{7}$ inch.

Genus DIPLOTROCHA, *Schmarda* (131).

Formed by Herr Schmarda to receive a free-swimming Rotiferon, *D. ptygura*, found at Cairo. Its pear-shaped body is surmounted by a short cylindrical head, and tapers, continuously with a wrinkled foot, to two short toes. The corona, according to Schmarda, consists of two complete parallel circles of cilia surrounding the upper and lower margins of the cylindrical head. There is a pair of long narrow teeth curved towards each other; a short circular stomach; and a red, semilunar, cervical eye. No other details are given, and no mention is made of the position of the mouth, so that it is impossible to say what this creature really was. As it was only about $\frac{1}{100}$ inch in length, it might have been some young Rhizotan. Schmarda's figure is of little value.

Genus DIURELLA, *Eyferth* (40).
Genus HETEROGNATHUS, *Schmarda* (135).

Each of these includes several genera of the family *Rattulidæ*. Of the latter, four species, viz. *brachydactylus, diglenus, macrodactylus, notommata,* said to be new, are given by Schmarda; but see note 1, Sup', p. 8. Of the former, *tigris* and *rattulus* have been mentioned vol. ii. pp. 65, 67; while *stylata* (40), and *insignis* (Herrick, 175), I cannot determine.

Genus HYDRIAS, *Ehrenberg* (12).

This genus contains one species, *cornigera*, a Philodine without eyes, proboscis, or spurs; and with its corona divided into two separate circles of cilia, each placed on a separate projection of the body. This kind of corona has been attributed, by numerous observers, to various Rotifera that do not possess it: in fact, no such corona is known. Ehrenberg found this Rotiferon in standing water in Africa; but it is too imperfectly observed to be admitted.

Genus MACROTRACHELA, *Milne* (186).

Mr. Milne proposes this genus for three-toed *Philodinadæ*, having the pre-intestinal part of the body decidedly longer than the post-anal. All the species are *Callidina* and have already been described (see Index), except *musculosa* and *tridens*, which are doubtful species.

Genus MONOLABIS, *Ehrenberg* (12).

This genus of Ehrenberg is intended to contain such *Philodinadæ* as have no proboscis, but have two frontal eyes, and a spurless foot with two small toes. There are two species, *conica* and *gracilis*; the former has the shape of a stout flattened cone, tapering to a foot continuous with the body, and bearing two minute toes; the latter is of similar shape, but much more narrow and slender. *Conica* has three transverse teeth in each ramus, and a *ventral* antenna: *gracilis* has two transverse teeth in each ramus, but no antenna at all.

It is obvious that whatever these Rotifera may have been, they were not *Philodinadæ*. The absence of the proboscis, of the characteristic sliding joints in the foot and body, and of the spurs on the foot, sufficiently show this. Possibly they were young Rhizotans; but the ascription, to one of them, of a single *ventral* antenna, makes it more than probable that the animals were imperfectly observed.

Genus NOTOGONIA, *Perty* (121).

The only species, *N. Ehrenbergii* (Pl. XXXIII. fig. 38), has a lorica widening backwards from the front, and with its hind edge bounded by three concave curves. A three-jointed foot bears two bristle-like toes. Perty draws an oval mastax and says that the jaws are "rounded and strong"; and the teeth, "two or three." The two eyes are wide apart in front, "very small and faintly red." He describes also, and figures, a pair of curved organs which protruded frequently from the front of the head.
Length, $\frac{1}{120}$ inch. **Habitat.** Near Belp (Perty).

Genus OTOGLENA, *Ehrenberg* (12).

Ehrenberg defined his genus *Otoglena* as containing animals, of his family *Hydatinæa*, with one sessile cervical eye, two stalked frontal eyes, and the foot forked. The genus included only one species, viz. *O. papillosa*, and I have little doubt from his description that it was a male Rotiferon, possibly that of *A. myrmeleo*, to the female of which Rotiferon he himself says it had much resemblance. The **body** was bell-shaped, swollen, and rough with papillæ; the **trophi** were apparently absent; the **vascular system** was obvious; the red cervical **eye** was attached to an oval nervous ganglion with two dark appendages; there was a long loop in the neck, and what Ehrenberg calls a "respiratory opening" in the middle of the back, but which no doubt was one of the usual setiferous pits in which the antennæ often end. Ehrenberg says that there was a somewhat clotted **stomach**, and a very thin intestine; but probably these were the **sperm-sac** and penis. The **foot** was conical, small, with very small toes. Ehrenberg never met with it but once.
Length, $\frac{1}{98}$ inch. **Habitat.** Berlin (Ehr.)

Genus PLAGIONATHA, *Dujardin* (40).

In this genus Dujardin places together *Notommata lacinulata*, *Distemma setigerum*, *Rattulus tigris*, *Diglena catellina*, *Notops hyptopus*, &c.: on account of a supposed similarity in their trophi.

Genus TETRASIPHON, *Ehrenberg*.

In Pritchard's *Infusoria* (4th edition, 1861) the following description is given of *T. hydrocora*, the only species of the genus. "Very large, hyaline, with two prominent tubular occipital organs, and other two near the termination of the back; gastric glands four, globose; jaws bidentate, with the oblique rotary organ of *Pleurotrocha*. Foot with slender, long, and acute toes; eye occipital. **Length**, $\frac{3}{40}$ inch, and upwards. Berlin."
It is possible that this may have been *Copeus spicatus*; for although the latter has only *two* gastric glands, yet each of these is so deeply divided into two lobes, that there often seem to be four. On the other hand, the trophi of *C. spicatus* are not bidentate; moreover no mention is made of the gelatinous covering, in which *spicatus* is so often enveloped.

Genus THEORUS, *Ehrenberg* (42).

A genus founded on the presence of two groups of supposed eyes, in the neck of a Notommatoid Rotiferon. Ehrenberg describes these so-called eye-points as colourless vesicles, but it is most improbable that they should be eyes at all. There were as many as six vesicles in each group. Mr. Milne (186) has seen a similar group of vesicles in each of the gastric glands of his *Stephanops uncinatus*.

Genus TYPHLINA, *Ehrenberg* (12).

The only species, *T. viridis*, was found by Ehrenberg at Cairo. He describes it as a very small animal, $\frac{1}{140}$ inch, without eyes, proboscis, or spurs, but with a sessile corona.

Genus TYPHLOTROCHA, *Schmarda* (135).

The only species, *T. zygodonta*, was found by Schmarda, in standing water, at S. Juan del Norte, Central America; and was placed by him among the *Hydatinæa*. It is somewhat like *Floscularia campanulata*. The body is nearly cylindrical; is surmounted in front by a five-lobed funnel-shaped cup, and terminated behind by a long toe-less narrow foot. Schmarda says nothing of the approach to the alimentary canal (so striking a part of the structure of the Floscules), but merely notices that the lobes are closely edged with cilia, of which two are very long. He says that the mastax is a transverse ellipsoid; and that the ovary stretches down to the bottom of the long foot. It is hardly possible that all these statements should be correct.

ADDENDA.

FLOSCULARIA CORONETTA, (var.). Mr. Thos. Whitelegge found, in 1885, in Sydney, N.S.W., a variety of *coronetta* which had the tips of its lobes, on their inner sides, expanded into flat discs. The figure (Pl. XXXIV. fig. 1) I owe to the courtesy of Mr. W. Burne Poole, who found the creature in a small pond in the Botanical Gardens ot Adelaide.

FURCULARIA GAMMARI, *Plate* (209), (Pl. XXXIV. fig. 8). An ecto-parasite discovered by Dr. Plate on the branchial laminæ of *Gammarus pulex*. There is nothing remarkable in its structure except a pair of unusually long foot-glands.

CORRIGENDA.

Vol. i., p. 91, l. 32; for *Cephalosiphon* read *Conochilus*.

Vol. ii., p. 7, l. 40; under T. BREVISETA, *Gosse*, place (Pl. XIII. fig. 7.)

Vol. ii., p. 47, l. 32; for (Pl. XVII. fig. 14) read (Pl. XVII. fig. 10.)

BIBLIOGRAPHY OF THE ROTIFERA.

(Continued from vol. ii. p. 142.)

162. Beneden, P. J. van,
    et Hesse, C. E. §*Recherches sur les Bdellodes ou Hirudinées, et les Trematodes marins*, Brussels, 1863.
163. Blagg, J. W. . . *Philodina citrina* (var.), Science Gossip, 1887, p. 67.
164. Bourne, A. C. . . '*Rotifera*,' Encyclop. Britan., xxi., 1886, p. 4.
165. Daday, E. von . *Hexarthra polyptera*, Természetraj. Füzetek. x., Budapest, 1886.
166. Eckstein, C. . . *Callidina symbiotica*, Zool. Anzeig., Oct. 1888.
167. Eichwald, E. v. . *D. erste Nachtrag zur Infusorienkunde*, Bull. Soc. Mosc., xx., 1847.
168. Forel, F. A. . . §*La Faune profonde des Lacs Suisses*, Mém. d. l. Soc. Helv. d. Sci. Nat. xxix., 1885, p. 81.
169. Gosse, P. H. . . *Twenty-four new species of Rotifera*, Journ. Roy. Micr. Soc., 1887, p. 1.
170.   „   „   . . *Twelve new species of Rotifera*, Journ. Roy. Micr. Soc., 1887, p. 361.
171.   „   „   . . *Twenty-four more new species of Rotifera*, Journ. Roy. Micr. Soc. 1887, p. 861.
172. Grube, E. . . . §*Genus Scison. Ein Ausflug nach Triest u. d. Quarnero*, Berlin, 1861.
173. Guerne, J. de . *On the Asplanchnadæ*, transl. in Ann. Nat. Hist., July 1888, p. 28.
174. Hartmann, R. . §*Üb. ein. Räderth. d. Griebnitzsees bei Neu-Babelsberg*, Sitzungsber. Gesellschaft, Nat. Fr., 1885, N 2, p. 19.
175. Herrick, C. L. . *Notes on American Rotifers*, Bull. Sci. Lab. Denison Univ., i., 1885, p. 43.
176. Hood, J. . . . *Synchæta gyrina*, Science Gossip, 1887, p. 149.
177.   „   „   . . *Synchæta longipes*, Science Gossip, 1887, p. 220.
178. Hudson, C. T. . *Foreign Rotifera*, Nature, 7 March, 1889 ; and Journ. Roy. Micr. Soc., 1889, p. 160.
179. Imhof, O. E. . . *Üb. d. pelag. Fauna d. Süsswasserbecken*, &c., Zool. Anzeig., 1887-8.
180. Kellicott, D. S. . *Floscularia Millsii*, Proc. Amer. Soc. Micr., 1885, p. 48.
181.   „   „   . . *Partial list of Rotifera of Shiawassee river*, Proc. Amer. Soc. Micr. 1888.
182. Levinsen, G. M. R. §*Nogle bemärkinger om Grønlands Rotatoriefauna*, Vidensk. Meddl. fra. Naturh. Foren. Kjøbenhavn, 1881, p. 181.
183. Lord, J. E. . . *A prolific pond*, Science Gossip, 1887, p. 185.
184.   „   „   . . *Notholca scapha*, Science Gossip, 1887, p. 207.
185.   „   „   . . *Notes on the genera Euchlanis and Colurus*, Science Gossip, 1886, pp. 83, 195.
186. Milne, W. . . . *Defectiveness of eye-spot in Philodinæa*, Phil. Soc. Glasgow, 1885 6.
187.   „   „   . . *Rotifer as a parasite, or tube-dweller*, Phil. Soc. Glasgow, 1888-9.
188.   „   „   . . *Diglena mustela*, Phil. Soc. Glasgow, 1884-5, p. 188.
189. Nordqvist, O. . . *Die pelagische u. Tiefseefauna d. grösseren finnischen Seen*, Zool. Anzeig., 1887, pp. 339, 358.
190. Pavesi . . . . §*Altra serie di recherche e studi sulla fauna pelagica dei laghi Italiani*, Padova, 1883.
191. Plate, L. . . . *Callidina parasitica*, &c., Sieb. u. Köll. Zeits., 1885 6, xliii., p. 229.
192.   „   . . . . *Parascison asplanchnus*, &c., transl. in Ann. Nat. Hist., July, 1887.
193. Plessis, G. du . §*La faune profonde des lacs de la Suisse*, Mém. d. l. Soc. Helv. d. Sci. Nat., xxix., 1885, Bâle.
194. Rousselet, C. . . *Synchæta infested with Trichodina*, Science Gossip, 1887, p. 43.
195.   „   „   . . *Asplanchna myrmeleo*, Science Gossip, 1888, p. 172.
196.   „   „   . . *Limnias cornuella*, Journ. Queh. Micr. Club, 1889, p. 337.
197. Stokes, A. C. . . *Rotifer within an Acanthocystis*, The Microscope, 1884, p. 33.
198. Tessin, G. . . . *Üb. Eibildung u. Entwicklung d. Rotatorien*, Sieb. u. Köll. Zeits., xliv., 1886, p. 273.
199. Weber, F. F. . . *Rotateurs des environs de Genève*, Arch. d. Biol., viii., 1888, p. 647.
200. Western, G. . . *Asplanchna myrmeleo* (male), Science Gossip, 1888, p. 256.
201. Zacharias, O. . . *Stephanops Leydigii*, Sieb. u. Köll. Zeits., 1885-6, xliii., p. 255 ; and Zool. Anzeig., 1886, p. 318.
202.   „   „   . . *D. pelag. Fauna norddeutscher Seen*, Zool. Anzeig., 1886, p. 564.
203.   „   „   . . *Revivification of Rotatoria*, Biol. Centralbl., vi., 1886, p. 230.
204.   „   „   . . *Fauna of Eifel-Maare*, Ann. Nat. Hist., March, 1889, p. 292.
205. Zelinka, C. . . *Callidina symbiotica*, &c., Sieb. u. Köll. Zeits., xliv., 1886, p. 396.
206.   „   „   . . *Discopus Synaptæ*, Arb. a. d. Zool. Inst. zu Graz, 1888, p. 141.
207. Daday, E. von . *Asplanchna triophthalma*, and *Schizocerca diversicornis*, Budapest, 1885.
208.   „   „   . . *Brachionus budapestinensis*, Természetraj. Füzetek, Budapest, ix., 1885.
209. Plate, L. . . . *Furcularia gammari*, Sieb. u. Köll. Zeits., 1885-6, xliii., p. 236.
210. Vorce, C. M. . . *Gomphogaster areolatus*, Proc. Amer. Soc. Microscopists, 1887.

INDEX OF THE FAMILIES, GENERA, AND SPECIES DESCRIBED IN THE SUPPLEMENT.

PLATE XXXI.

1. Philodina microps . . a, dorsal view; b, lateral.
2. Callidina pigra . . . dorsal view.
3. Asplanchna eupoda . . lateral view.
4. Synchæta longipes . . dorsal view.
5. Taphrocampa selenura . . dorsal view.
6. Notommata limax . . a, dorsal view; b, lateral; c, brain and eye.
7. Notommata ovulum . . dorsal view.
8. Notommata theodora. . a, dorsal view; b, lateral.
9. Notommata potamis . . dorsal view.
10. Proales coryneger . . dorsal view.
11. Proales othodon . . . dorsal view.
12. Proales prehensor . . a, dorsal view; b, lateral.
13. Furcularia lactistes . . a, dorsal view; b, lateral.
14. Furcularia molaris . . dorsal view.
15. Furcularia sterea . . dorsal view.
16. Furcularia sphærica . . dorsal view.
17. Furcularia eva . . . a, lateral view; b, dorsal.
18. Furcularia melandocus . a, dorsal view; b, toes.
19. Furcularia lophyra . . lateral view.
20. Diglena aquila . . . a, dorsal view; b, lateral.
21. Diglena rosa . . . dorsal view.
22. Diglena silpha . . . lateral view.
23. Diglena pachida . . ventral view.
24. Diglena snilla . . . lateral view.
25. Distemma platyceps . . lateral view.
26. Mastigocerca iernis . . a, lateral view; b, base of toes.
27. Mastigocerca bicristata . lateral view.
28. Dinschiza fretalis . . a, dorsal view; b, trophi, lateral; c, trophi, dorsal.
29. Dinschiza acronota . . lateral view.
30. Dinschiza globata . . a, lateral view; b, dorsal.
31. Dinschiza cupha . . a, lateral view; b, toe, lateral.
32. Dinschiza ramphigera . a, lateral view; b, trophi, dorsal; c, trophi, lateral.
33. Salpina marina . . . lateral view.
34. Euchlanis oropha . . a, lateral view; b, transverse section.
35. Dapidia stroma . . . lorica; a, lateral view; b, ventral; c, posterior.
36. Cathypna ungulata . . lorica; a, anterior occipital edge; b, anterior mental;
                          c, base of toes; d, toes.
37. Cathypna latifrons . . . dorsal view.
38. Cathypna diomis . . . a, base of lorica, foot and toes, dorsal view; b, toes, lateral.
39. Distyla lipara . . . . dorsal view.
40. Distyla striata . . . . dorsal view.
41. Monostyla mollis . . . dorsal view.
42. Colurus dicentrus . . . a, lateral view; b, ditto, enlarged.
43. Colurus grallator . . . lateral view.
44. Colurus dumnonius . . a, dorsal view; b, lateral.
45. Colurus micromela . . a, lateral; b, transverse section.
46. Colurus leptus . . . . lateral view.
47. Metopidia pygmæa . . a, dorsal view; b, transverse section.
48. Dispinthera capsa . . a, dorsal view; b, lateral.
49. Monura bartonia . . . lateral view.
50. Monura loncheres . . . lateral view.
51. Mytilia pœcilops . . . a, dorsal view; b, lateral.
52. Mytilia teresa . . . . dorsal view.
53. Mytilia producta . . . a, dorsal view; b, lateral.
54. Pterodina reflexa . . . posterior view.
55. Anuræa schista . . . a, dorsal view; b, lateral.
56. Notholca labis . . . . a, dorsal view; b, lateral.
57. Notholca spinifera . . . dorsal view.
58. Notholca rhomboidea . . dorsal view.
59. Notholca jugosa . . . . dorsal view.
60. Notholca polygona . . . dorsal view.

₊ All these figures were drawn by Mr. Gosse to illustrate his three papers (169, 170, 171) in the Journ. Roy. Micr. Soc., 1887.

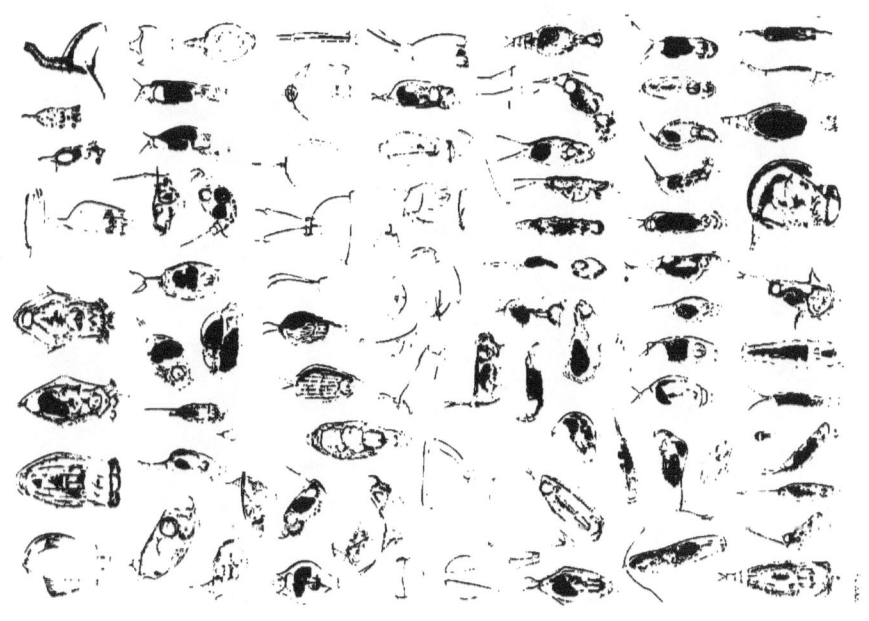

PLATE XXXII.

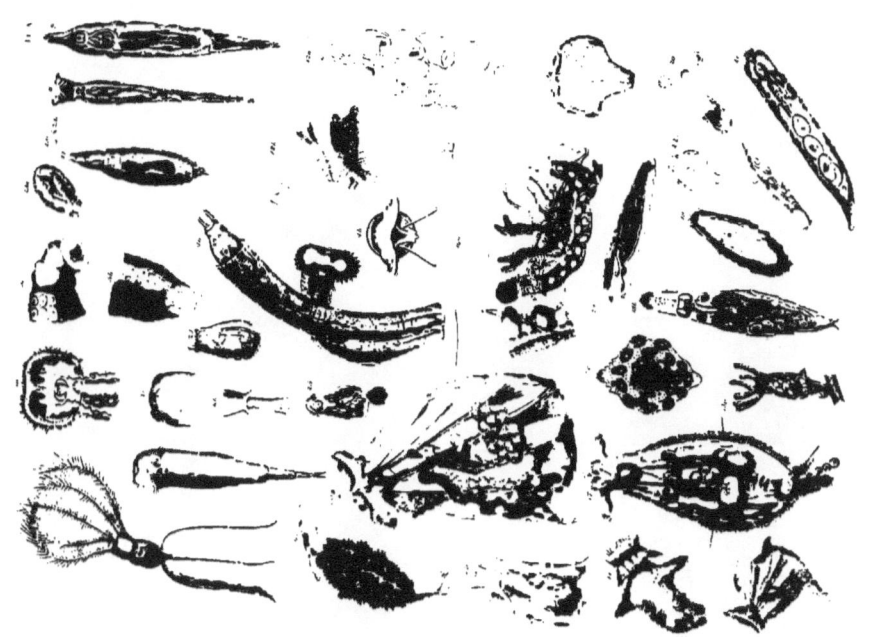

PLATE XXXIII.

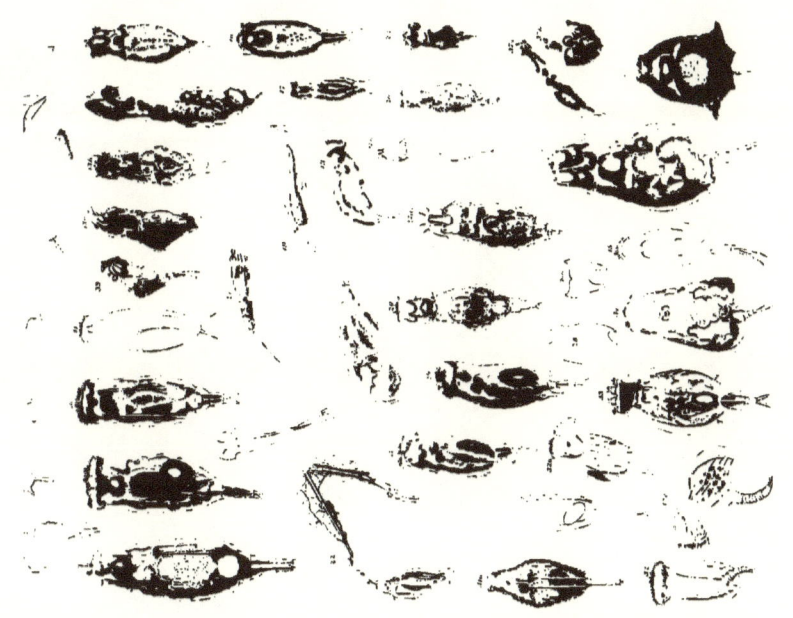

PLATE XXXIV.